D1297450

PAWSITIVEILY HOME FOR CHRISTMAS

CHRISTMAS IN SNOWY FALLS BOOK 2

JACQUELINE WINTERS

Copy Editor: Write Girl Editing Services

Cover Design: Blue Valley Author Services

Proofreading: FictionEdit.com

CHAPTER 1

HLOE

CHLOE TAGGERT INHALED DEEPLY, fighting panic the best she could as crisp snowflakes crunched beneath her quickly moving feet. There simply wasn't enough time on the clock. She had to make five stops on her way to Bangor before she picked up her latest rescue pup, and Grandma was promising a blizzard. "Blasted Reindeer Bingo," she mumbled with a laugh, stuffing the last box of homemade dog treats in the back seat of her van.

If it hadn't been for Grandma Annie's insistence that Chloe take her to the holiday bingo event last night, she might've snuck in another hour of sleep and already been thirty miles down the road. *At least Grandma Annie took home the jackpot.*

Chloe hurried back for the duffle bag sitting right inside the front door, checking every jacket pocket with a quick pat before she locked up. Even if Grandma Annie was wrong about the snowstorm that no weather forecaster was predicting, Chloe would need to stay the night somewhere. She hated driving home in the dark on icy roads. Add in an excessively energetic dog, and the decision to stay overnight was a no-brainer.

"Good morning, Chloe!" her neighbor Tricia Anderson called with a wave from her mailbox.

"It *is* a good morning, isn't it?" Chloe returned with a chipper smile, sliding the van door closed but stopping halfway. She reached inside one of the carefully packed boxes, retrieving a bag of sweet potato dog treats for Mitzy. Chloe adored her neighbor, who'd moved to town three years ago for a third-grade teaching job, and happily sacrificed five minutes. Small price for the times Tricia allowed Chloe to bring a rescue into her classroom to demonstrate how rewarding adopting a dog in need of a good home could be.

Tricia met Chloe on the sidewalk connecting their houses. In only a long-sleeved button-up shirt, leggings, and a green striped stocking hat, Tricia appeared comfortable, whereas Chloe would've been a Popsicle. "Can you believe it? In less than forty-eight hours, *both* of my kids and my granddaughter will be home for Christmas. I can't wait for Kaylee to meet Mitzy. I'm so glad you found her for me. Couldn't ask for a better dog."

"Mitzy will absolutely love your granddaughter." Chloe handed over a bag of the Yorkie's favorite treats. "She's great with kids."

"Any word on your family?" Tricia asked.

Chloe's entire family, outside of her brother Noah, who'd shown up for a surprise visit just yesterday, was in Cancun trying to talk her youngest sister out of eloping. They were due home before Christmas, unless a snowstorm impeded their travel plans. "No updates yet, but I'm optimistic they'll make it for the tree lighting on Christmas Eve."

"Your mother's a saint," Tricia said, a half smile on her lips. "I thought two kids were a handful, but *seven*?"

Discreetly, Chloe glanced at her watch. She had no problem speeding her way to Bangor during the summer, but between the black ice and occasional moose, the roads weren't trustworthy this time of year. "To be fair, most of us are well-behaved." Chloe gave a wink. "Just my little sister who's being a pain in the neck."

Mitzy let out an eager bark from the window, perched on the back of the couch, all too aware of the prize Tricia held in her hands. Tricia turned, taking a step toward home, but then stopped to ask, "Headed off to pick up another rescue?"

"Last trip to Bangor before Christmas." Though Chloe picked up rescues from all over, she made the six-hour drive to the Bangor airport at least once every couple of months for special circumstances. She fished her phone from a coat pocket and scrolled through her email until she found Belle's profile. "Got a bundle of energy on the way," she said with a chuckle, handing over the phone.

"She looks like a sweetheart."

"If by *sweetheart* you mean notorious for destroying dog beds and tearing down wallpaper . . ."

"Oh, my. You don't have wallpaper in there, do you?" Tricia nodded at Chloe's rented ranch.

"A little. But I've been begging my brother to let me rip it down. Belle might speed up the process." She dropped the phone back in her pocket. "She's not the first Energizer Bunny I've taken in. I've got a few tricks up my sleeve." If only she had someone in mind to adopt Belle. *All in good time.*

"You're a wonderful person, Chloe. Just think of how many dogs have good homes because you refused to give up on them." Tricia raised the dog treat bag in her palm. "I'll leave a check in your mailbox."

"Not necessary. Merry Christmas, Tricia."

"But I want to. I know how important opening your rescue facility is. At least let me make a donation. It's the least I can do after all the treats you donated to Parker's unit. Both those dogs are in heaven because of you."

"I was happy to send them." Tricia's son, Parker, was currently serving a deployment in Afghanistan. Though he himself wasn't a dog handler, there were a couple of bomb-sniffing dogs in his unit.

"I know they're appreciated," Tricia added, "which is why I want to donate to your future shelter. I think your idea is wonderful! Just think of how many more dogs you'll be able to help once it's up and running."

Chloe's heart warmed at her neighbor's generosity. While a part-time medical billing job paid the bills and let her work from home, she'd spent the past several years investing in her dream. Making dog treats, dog beds, and dog toys in the hopes that her profits would eventually allow her to open a rescue shelter of her own. "Thank you. That means a lot."

Mitzy yipped again, this time snappier. "Guess I better get these inside before she has a fit." Three steps away, Tricia turned again. "Maybe you'll run into Parker while you're at the airport. He gets in this afternoon. I bet you'll recognize him from all the pictures I force on you. He'll be wearing an army uniform," she added, and Chloe heard the emotion in her voice. She knew Tricia'd really wanted to be there at the airport, to welcome him home properly.

"I'll keep my eyes peeled for him," Chloe

promised, waving once to officially seal it, and then hustled the last few steps to her van.

"Have a safe drive!" Tricia called and, to Mitzy's apparent relief, finally stepped inside her house.

Chloe rubbed her hands together in the driver's seat, happy that the van had adequate time to warm up. As it was, she'd have to forego one, maybe two, of her stops today. "There's always tomorrow." *With a wallpaper-loving, Energizer Bunny in tow.*

SEVEN HOURS, three gift shop drop-offs, and one lunch stop later, Chloe pulled into the Bangor International Airport. A quick check of the itinerary pinned on her phone confirmed that Belle's flight had landed twenty minutes prior. By now, they should have the dog unloaded and ready for her to sign for.

Stuffing a leash and bag of dog treats in her purse, Chloe hurried toward the baggage claim office.

Belle was a loveable dog, from what she'd been told on the phone. But 'handful' didn't begin to describe the complaints from three former owners.

Chloe was no stranger to overly energetic dogs. Often, she found the previous owners simply didn't have a lifestyle conducive to the amount of exercise such a dog required. Many found themselves frustrated when dog beds, furniture, and shoes ended up destroyed.

Weaving her way through a mob of people, Chloe heard sharp, impatient yipping followed by a long howl. *Hold on, Belle. I'm coming.*

But, apparently, Belle just couldn't *Hold On*. No sooner did Chloe turn the corner, heading for the office, than she caught a blur of black and white fur charging her way. Besides the energy, she'd been warned that Belle was a bit of an escape artist. "Belle!" she called, pivoting on the ball of her foot to chase after the dog. *A bit of an escape artist, huh?*

The husky-shepherd mix caused shrieks all the way down the long corridor, people jumping out of the way as Chloe sprinted after her. "Belle!"

She pushed down on her panic as Belle charged toward a revolving door. Chloe hated to think what might happen if the dog escaped into outside traffic. She ran faster, purse banging against her hip the whole way. The stashed treats were worthless if she couldn't catch up to the runaway canine.

A woman crouched down, calling to the dog. Belle darted around her at the last minute.

"Pete wasn't kidding about this one," Chloe muttered, the stitch in her side stabbing with every step.

A tall man in gray camo stepped into Belle's path, hand lifted like an old-time traffic cop in the classic *halt* gesture. He let out a loud whistle, effec-

7

tively turning the heads of every person not already invested in the incident, and getting even the dog's attention. Belle's paws shuffled beneath her as she tried, and failed, to stop on the slippery floor. On her butt, the dog slid right into the soldier.

Both of them went down.

Chloe made it to their side seconds later.

"Got her!" the solider announced, hand looped through her collar.

"Belle, *what* were you thinking?" Chloe scolded, though concern trumped her anger by a mile. The relief that Belle hadn't successfully made it outside hit Chloe in a wave. She grabbed the leash from her purse and dropped to her knees, clipping it on her pink collar.

"This your dog?" the soldier asked, still flat on his back and petting Belle.

"She's a rescue," Chloe explained, flashing him a smile of gratitude. His sapphire gaze met her own, causing her heart to skip a beat. He looked familiar. "I'm fostering her until I find a good home. A forever home." She stood, reaching a hand out to the soldier, careful to avoid those eyes. They felt . . . dangerous, yet safe. Chloe didn't understand the jumble of contradicting emotions and pushed them away.

"Quite a handful you've got there."

"Tell me about it." Chloe wiggled her fingers at him, repeating the offer of a helping hand.

Finally, he accepted her help. His larger hand

felt warm against her own icy fingers. An odd sense of comfort washed over her at his touch. "Try putting the leash on *before* you let her out of the crate next time?" The soldier winked at her.

Chloe let out a heavy sigh, happy she'd caught her breath again. Running was among her least favorite pastimes. "I'll remember that, Sergeant"—she glanced at the name tag on his uniform—"Anderson." She shook her head with a laugh. "Any chance your name is *Parker* Anderson?"

"How did—"

"I thought you looked vaguely familiar. I've only seen about a hundred photos. Your mom is my neighbor."

"In Snowy Falls?"

"That's the one." She nodded as Belle pushed against her hand, demanding pats. It seemed that if Chloe kept her fingers moving along the dog's soft fur, Belle wasn't as eager to bolt. "Your mom's excited to have you home for Christmas this year. I mean like *really* excited. Your bed's been made for a week and the kitchen is fully stocked with—well, I can't tell you. It's a surprise."

"I guess I'll be seeing more of you, *neighbor*."

Chloe spotted an airport worker headed her way, waving a clipboard. "I better get Belle's crate."

"Has she been on a plane long?" Parker asked, nodding at the dog.

"Six hours or more."

9

"I could run her outside for you while you get all that sorted."

Chloe beamed a smile at him. "Would you?"

"Been a long time since I've had a dog. I don't mind." It wasn't until Chloe caught herself staring into those eyes that Parker cleared his throat and added, "Meet you back here?"

"Sounds good." She spun toward the airport agent headed her way, a useless attempt to hide the blush creeping up her neck. The cell phone pictures Tricia had forced on Chloe over the years didn't do the man justice. *He's a soldier home for a short holiday break. He's* not *staying.* The words did nothing to slow the erratic beating of her heart.

CHAPTER 2

ARKER

THE DOG WASN'T the only one following Chloe down the airport corridor with a lingering gaze. Parker slung his duffle bag over one shoulder and led Belle outside. "C'mon girl."

What are the odds? Meeting someone from Snowy Falls, and his mom's neighbor no less, in *this* airport. It wasn't a drive he'd ask his mom to make in the summer, much less with two feet of snow on the ground. It was the reason he insisted on driving a rental car home.

Parker found a patch of snow-covered grass for Belle and waited.

Chloe's soft blonde curls remained forefront in his mind, right along with her radiant smile. He sucked in a deep breath and did his best to push away the image. Neighbor or not, the last thing he needed was to get hung up on a woman.

Parker was on a mission: get into the Special Forces, just like his dad. With that goal so close to being achieved, he heeded the advice of his commander and kept himself unattached. He was visiting to spend time with family, not to get entangled in a romance.

Belle let out a bark and tugged on the leash, aiming for an open field.

"C'mon, girl," he said again, urging her back toward the revolving doors. "Chloe's waiting for you." Only, she hadn't returned yet. He wasn't certain of the paperwork required to pick up a dog. So he walked Belle to the rental counter instead.

"Is she a service dog?" a woman behind the counter asked, her voice nasally. She pushed up horn rimmed glasses with her index finger.

Parker raised an eyebrow at that, certain the woman witnessed the incident that happened less than ten minutes prior. He'd been tackled a few feet from the rental counter, turning most heads in this wing of the airport. "No."

"Where's her crate?"

Catching a distant glimpse of Chloe pushing a

dog crate on a cart, he hooked a thumb in her direction. "On its way."

"Dogs aren't allowed out of their crates in the airport."

Parker turned away and scrubbed a hand over his face, doing his best to maintain a smile, even if it was forced. Getting leave for Christmas while deployed to Afghanistan was nothing short of a miracle. Simple luck that his original date was needed by an expectant father, which allowed for a rarely approved trade. But since his departure from the FOB, he'd faced one delay after another. Already, he'd eaten three days of his leave in a variety of airports. He was tired, and his patience was thin.

"Sir?" the woman said.

Turning back, he said, "I need to rent a car."

"What about the dog? You can't have her in a rental car."

Parker leaned on the counter, pushed past the fatigue, and laid on the charm. He flashed a smile that often got his way in non-military situations. "She's not riding with me. What kind of car can I get?"

The woman's expression softened in a second. She finally relaxed her pursed lips and something close to a blush spread along her cheeks. "Let me check—"

"We're out of cars," a balding man announced, popping out of the cramped office.

"Out?" Parker and the woman said in unison.

"I'm sorry, sir," the man with a manager placard pinned to his shirt said. He hooked both thumbs behind a maroon vest, running them up and down as if the vest were suspenders. "We won't have any more cars for two days. Same with everyone else, it seems." With an apologetic shrug, he added, "Holidays, you know."

Parker scanned the rental counters on either side, but witnessed people receiving the same news. If he had any faith in his arrival time, Parker would've made a reservation. "No cars at all?"

The manager shook his head.

"What about a bus?" Though he highly doubted any bus would get him close to his mom's small town.

"There's one headed to Springfield but it left ten minutes ago. Next one isn't until tomorrow."

"Is there a problem?" Chloe's voice, sweet as an angel, cut through the tension. For a single moment, Parker felt his worries dissipate. He didn't understand it. She took Belle's leash from him, her chilly fingertips brushing the back of his hand, and looked at him expectantly.

He gave her a helpless shrug, catching a glimpse of the battered dog crate that'd never again contain a dog. *Impressive, Belle.* "No rental cars for two days."

"You can ride with me," Chloe offered. "But I have to warn you, I'm stopping in Hollandale for the night. You won't make it home until lunchtime tomorrow."

"You wouldn't mind an extra passenger?"

"You've *met* Belle, right? I could use the help."

Parker's immediate instinct was to say *yes*, and that startled him. Chloe already had an effect on him he couldn't explain. Would spending another twenty-four hours with her be wise? But his alternative was to get a hotel room and hope a rental car came available a couple of days from now. Christmas was only four days away as it was.

"You're sure it's no trouble?"

"I'm sure if your mother found out I left you here, she wouldn't be too happy with me."

"You're right," he agreed. "You'll at least let me pay for gas?"

Chloe let out a cute laugh. "Well, I'm not going to argue if that's what you mean. C'mon. I want to get all this loaded up before I have to pay for my parking spot." She glanced at her watch. "I have twelve minutes to scoot. Didn't bank on the extracurriculars."

"Have a Merry Christmas," the rental manager said, still an apologetic smile on his face. "Thank you for your service."

Parker nodded his thanks and stepped behind the cart before Chloe could.

"I can get that," she said.

"Mom wouldn't be too happy with me if I wasn't

the gentleman she raised me to be. You've got enough going on there with Houdini. You'll want both hands in case she tries anything else."

Already, Belle was walking in erratic zigzags as they headed toward the revolving doors. "Point taken."

He followed Chloe into the parking garage, surprised to find a gray van with the lavender wording *Chloe's K9 Creations* written on the side. It looked very familiar, but he couldn't place where he'd seen the logo before. "You have your own business?" he asked, nodding toward the lettering.

Chloe popped a back door open and he muscled the mangled crate behind the back seat. "I make dog treats, beds, blankets, toys. Stuff like that." She shut the door, wedging the crate between door and seat.

"*And* you rescue dogs?"

"More or less. I'm kind of a middleman when a shelter can't find a home for a dog. I take them in, see what I can do to help break bad habits, and then find them a match." He followed her to a side door. She handed Parker the leash so she could spread a folded blanket with several chewed holes in an open area.

"Interesting setup you have here." Parker poked his head inside, noticing the only seat besides the two buckets up front was the far one in the back. The others had been removed. Different totes were secured to the sides, making him curious what was inside. The middle area was open enough to hold two crates, but right now it was covered with a holey blanket.

"C'mon Belle," she said, taking the leash back.

Each graze of their fingers felt more like a spark of electricity. Parker fought the urge to shove his hands in his pockets since he was still in uniform. He was eager to change out of it first chance he got. Three days in the same clothes was enough.

"Looks like someone chewed up that blanket," he pointed out.

"That was Rocco. Then Birdie. Now it'll no doubt be Belle. I might have to throw the blanket out after we get home. I doubt it'll survive another wash cycle."

Parker studied Chloe a bit longer than he probably should, admiring the way her curls covered her shoulders. She wore snow boots—*smart*—and a long hunter green coat that went to her knees. Something about *her* felt very familiar too, but Parker couldn't place it. Mom had probably mentioned her in one conversation or another.

"Let me call Heidi to make sure she has an extra room." Chloe sank her hand into a massive coat pocket, pulling out a phone. "Why don't you get settled in the van? Keep Belle from chewing on the seat belts if you can."

Parker smiled at that, but Chloe's serious expression gave him little room to doubt her assessment.

Dropping into the passenger seat, he realized

he'd yet to text Mom and let her know about the most recent delay. By now, she should be used to the phone calls that promised little more than another setback. At least he was stateside. That in and of itself was an accomplishment.

He scrubbed his hand along the back of Belle's head, earning double-time tail wags. "You look so sweet and innocent. Hard to believe you caused all that commotion a few minutes ago."

With his free hand, he dug into a cargo pocket for his phone. Texting with both hands would be easier, but he felt safer keeping one hand on Belle. She seemed less apt to destroy things if she was receiving physical attention. He called Mom instead.

"Parker!" Mom answered on the first ring. "Did you make it to Bangor? Please tell me you're not still stuck in Germany."

"I'm in Bangor."

"Oh, good. What time do you think you'll be here? I can have supper—"

"Mom, I won't make it home today."

Her silence racked him with guilt, despite how none of the delays had been his fault. He'd missed Christmas the past three years in a row, ever since she moved to Snowy Falls, and Mom was looking forward to his visit more than any holiday festivity or tradition she treasured. "What now?"

"No rental cars or buses headed that way. But I met your neighbor, Chloe." He quickly added the last so Mom wouldn't have a chance to throw her keys in the tote bag she called a purse. "She's going to give me a ride."

"Oh, how wonderful!"

"We're stopping in some little town —Hollandaise?"

"Hollandale."

"Yeah, that's the one. We won't be in Snowy Falls until tomorrow."

He waited for Mom's disappointment, but instead she sounded delighted. "It's no bother, Parker. Chloe is a sweetheart. Maybe this is Christmas magic!"

"Mom," Parker warned, watching Chloe outside the van as she paced on the phone. He'd have to take Mom off speaker at this rate. The last thing he needed was for her to get some matchmaking idea. He thought it best not to mention how Belle actually forced the introduction or she might get really carried away. "She's your neighbor, who generously offered me a ride. That's all this is."

"Okay." But her tone implied she believed the opposite. Parker shook his head.

"I'll shoot you a text when we're settled in for the night, okay?" he said. Chloe spun toward the van, no longer on the phone. "Gotta go, Mom. Talk to you later."

"Say hi to Chloe for me."

Parker ended the call half a second before the

driver's side door opened and Chloe hopped inside. "Good news. Heidi has one extra room," she told him. "Ready?"

After the arduous trip he'd endured, he was more than ready for a hearty meal and a comfortable bed. "Ready."

CHAPTER 3

HLOE

IN THE PAST couple of years, Chloe had become very familiar with the smaller towns along her route from Snowy Falls to Bangor. One her favorites, aside from her hometown, was Hollandale. It held more charm than all the others combined. Its friendliness, colorful Main Street buildings, Victorian-style houses, and enthusiasm for every holiday won her over the first time she stayed the night. Plus, they were much more dog-friendly than any other stop along the way.

"We'll get checked in, then grab a bite to eat," Chloe said, certain Parker had to be starving. Just listening to him recount his horrendous travel experience thus far made her stomach rumble.

"I'd eat just about anything right now." Parker let out a yawn. "Even an MRE sounds good."

"If I had more than homemade dog treats, I'd offer them up. I mean, they're edible—"

Parker let out a laugh. "Thanks, but I can wait for dinner."

Chloe turned onto a residential road and weaved her way up a steep hill, thankful her budget had afforded her new snow tires this year. Twice last winter, she'd had to park at the general store and ask Heidi, the inn's owner, to give her a lift.

Belle whined nervously as the motor worked harder. "We're almost there," Chloe reassured, thankful Parker was able to calm the dog with his pats since Chloe needed both of her hands on the wheel.

"Do all Maine towns have hills like this?" Parker asked.

"You haven't been to Maine before?"

"Not outside the Bangor airport," he admitted as Belle crawled into his lap and plastered herself against him. Parker held her with both arms, tucking her head against his shoulder. Chloe wondered what had caused the dog's anxiety and made a mental note about her behavior. "I hate to admit I haven't made it home for Christmas since Mom moved to Snowy Falls."

"She's extra happy to have you home this year." Chloe sensed Parker had a reason for his extended absence, most likely military related, but any inclination to ask about it would have to wait. "We're here." She put the van in park, peering through the windshield at a large, two-story, shingle-style home that'd been converted to a bed and breakfast a few years ago.

"You're sure there's a room for me?"

"There're ten guest rooms," Chloe explained, grabbing her purse from the floor and checking her phone. She shot a quick text to Grandma Annie, letting her know she made it to her lodging. She frowned at the low battery, promising herself she'd get it charging as soon as they settled in their rooms. "Heidi promised me one was still available for you."

Parker nodded, his hand falling to the door handle.

"Wait!" Chloe grabbed his arm, zings of electricity sparking under her fingertips from the unexpected contact. She dropped her hand almost instantly, shaking off the strange reaction as a combination of hunger and holiday bingo hangover. How many times had she told Grandma Annie it wasn't healthy to play two dozen consecutive rounds of bingo?

"We're not going in?" His eyebrows drew in confusion, apparently unaffected.

Chloe clipped Belle's leash onto her collar,

studying the dog instead of meeting Parker's curious gaze. The dog's eyes were wide, curiosity and excitement creating a booty wiggle even as she sat in Parker's lap. "She's a notorious escape artist," she reminded. "Aren't you, girl?" Chloe let out a giggle when Belle gave her a cold, wet nose to the cheek. "It's not safe to open a door if she isn't secured first."

Parker rubbed Belle along the neck. "Gotcha. Got to keep a close eye on you, don't we?"

The way he comforted Belle, speaking to her like a friend, melted Chloe's heart. If she didn't know better, she'd think Parker was the one destined to give the dog a forever home. "How long do you have left in the army?" she asked, hoping her tone sounded casual, nonchalant even, as she fished a treat from her purse. At the crinkling sound of the bag, Belle turned in Parker's lap and stuck her nose into Chloe's purse.

"Hard to say," Parker answered, getting a grip on the leash. "At least another decade, I guess. Maybe longer."

"You must love what you do." She masked her disappointment behind interest. She was rarely wrong about these things, but if Parker was going to be in the service that long, Belle was definitely the wrong dog for him. She needed someone who was home more than they weren't, and could see that she received adequate exercise daily.

"My dad was Army. Kind of runs in the family."

Now that Belle was secured with a leash and her attention was focused on the treat-filled purse, Chloe pushed open her door. She nodded at Parker to do the same, Belle slipping from lap to ground in a fluid hop.

Chloe waited at the bottom of the porch steps, watching Parker grab his duffle bag from the back and cover the walkway in a few strides. Belle trotted along at his side, not a care in the world or single eager tug on the leash. *Fascinating.*

The aroma of freshly baked cookies—snickerdoodle if her nose was correct—greeted them the moment the door opened.

"Those smell like heaven," Parker said.

Chloe winked at him over her shoulder. "They taste like it too."

"Chloe, so good to see you again!" Heidi popped out of her office situated beneath a rounded double staircase, both banisters wrapped in evergreen garland and shiny red ornaments. Her sweater, covered in decorated Christmas trees, matched the décor of the inn. "And this must be the soldier you told me about."

"Ma'am," Parker said with a nod, though Chloe noticed his eyes wandering the vaulted ceiling and custom woodwork, and landing on a fully decorated tree at least fifteen feet tall.

"Please, call me Heidi." Heidi peeked over the counter, spotting Belle. A massive smile illuminated her face as she came around and knelt in greeting. "You must be the escape artist I've heard *all* about." The best thing about staying at the B&B was Heidi's fierce love of dogs.

"Have a lot of guests?" Chloe asked, swiping a peppermint from the candy bowl on the front counter.

"Full after I get you both settled." Heidi pushed off her knee to stand, her silvering hair swishing and bell earrings jingling with her movements. "The only two I had left are adjoining rooms. Hope that won't be a problem. You can of course leave the doors locked on either side, but you'll share a bathroom."

Chloe warmed at the idea of having Parker close by. It made her feel safer, though she had nothing to be afraid of. It had to be the uniform. Or the familiarity. Maybe she didn't know Parker, but because of Tricia's stories and photos, she *felt* she did. "That'll be fine, Heidi. I appreciate you accommodating both of us so last minute."

Heidi lifted the two remaining keys from hooks on the wall beside the office door. "You kids decide who'll take which room. Makes no difference." She led them up one of the rounded staircases and headed toward the end of the hall before handing over the keys. "These two right here, eight and ten."

Belle sniffed at the doorknob of room eight, tail wagging, no doubt excited to explore another new area.

"No supper tonight," Heidi explained. "But there will be a hearty breakfast in the morning. Check out at eleven." She directed the last at Parker. "If either of you need a thing, just ring me." Heidi turned on her heel and rushed down the hall at the ringing of a landline. "Cookies in the dining room. Help yourself!"

Chloe held out both keys in offering. "I've stayed in every room she has," she explained.

"I have to decide blind, is that it?" Parker's smirk activated a butterfly or two in her stomach. "I'm taking the corner room, then. That should mean extra windows."

"Good choice."

Relinquishing Belle's leash to Chloe, Parker inserted the key into his door but stopped before he pushed it open. "Mind if I take a shower before we head off in search of food?"

"Go for it. Just knock when you're ready to go."

He looked at Belle. "Will she be okay in the room while we're gone?"

Chloe let out a hearty laugh at that. "With her résumé, not a chance. I wouldn't have a mattress to sleep on when we got back because she'd chew right through it. She'll come with us. Hollandale has a few dog-friendly restaurants, even in the winter months. It's why I stay here when I don't want to make the trip all in one day."

"I won't be long," Parker said, disappearing into

his room.

Once her own door was closed, Chloe unclipped Belle's leash and let her explore the room with her nose. "We'll get you some exercise after dinner," she promised. "I know just the place you can run free."

She dropped her purse onto the bed and searched it for her phone. She had a slew of texts from her best friend Everly that needed responses, but one look at her battery life holding at four percent reminded her she needed a charge more.

The silence, aside from the hiss of a shower, alerted Chloe to trouble. "Belle, why don't you come here?" The dog looked up at her from the corner of the bed, her eyes wide with innocence, the floral comforter in her mouth. "I have more of those treats you like."

Abandoning her plan of blanket destruction, Belle pounced at Chloe. "You have to sit," she told the dog. "Do you know how to—" Belle's butt plopped down so quickly the floorboards creaked. "Got that one down."

As Belle devoured her peanut butter dog biscuit, Chloe fished in her purse for a phone charger. "Oh, no." She dumped the contents onto the bed and barely stashed the treats before Belle took off with the bag. She had everything else she needed—billfold, mint lip balm, hair brush, extra pair of gloves, and her favorite author's latest cozy mystery in paperback.

But no phone charger.

Chloe pressed her lips together, deciding how to spend that last four percent—three now—before her phone died. She'd refused to upgrade her phone for years since hers worked perfectly fine. But whenever she forgot her charger—which happened more than she liked to admit—she couldn't count on anyone else to have the kind she needed. "Maybe Santa will upgrade my phone," she mumbled.

Belle pushed her head against Chloe's hand, demanding pats.

"No big deal, right? It's just a cell phone."

A gentle knock sent Belle darting across the room toward the bathroom door. She wedged her nose beneath the crack.

"Come in," Chloe called from the bed as she stuffed her dumped contents back in her purse.

"Whoa! Hey there, girl." Belle weaved through his legs like a cat on catnip. *Better than jumping, but still something to work on.* Parker bent over to offer some pets. It was when he stood back up that Chloe couldn't seem to peel her eyes away. He looked very different out of uniform. More relaxed and, if possible, more attractive. "I'm ready if you are."

Chloe cleared her throat, turning away as she shrugged back into her coat. *He's an attractive man, that's all.* But the butterflies in her stomach—waking one by one—had other things to say on the matter.

CHAPTER 4

ARKER

"IF YOU'RE A LOBSTER FAN, I recommend the lobster rolls." Chloe reached across the table, pointing to them on the menu. Belle leaned in to investigate, adding her nose to the party for good measure. Despite Chloe's best attempts to get the dog to lie on the floor beside the table—or even sit— she refused to stop fidgeting until Parker let her up into the booth seat. Oddly, no one in the restaurant seemed to bat an eye.

"I'm hungry enough to order one of everything on the menu," he said with a laugh, gently tugging Belle back by the collar. "Look, Miss Belle, if you're going to stay up here, you have to keep that eager nose of yours off the table."

The dog stared at him and, as if by some form of magic, seemed to understand. Belle laid down in the booth seat, her head resting in his lap. He dropped a hand to the ruff of her neck, massaging the base of one ear with his thumb. She sighed.

"She really likes you," Chloe said.

"She likes the prospect of handouts, no doubt." But Parker had to admit, in the few hours he'd spent with the dog, she'd already worn a soft spot in his heart. Too bad he could never adopt her. Having a dog while in the military had its own challenges, deployment aside. But once he became a Green Beret, having a dog would be a hindrance.

"How long have you been in the army?" Chloe asked after they placed their orders.

"Almost six years," he answered. He joined the summer before his dad passed away, but he didn't share that detail. Odd how compelled he felt to, though. He took a sip of soda instead.

Chloe thumbed through the laminated dessert menu. "What do you do, exactly? Your mom told me once, but I can't remember."

"Intelligence."

"Man of many words, huh?"

Parker let out a soft laugh. "It's . . . complicated."

"You should've said *top secret*. That sounds more mysterious and dangerous."

He was drawn to the twinkle in her emerald

31

eyes, realizing how easily he could lose himself in their depths. If only he allowed his guard to drop.

Parker cleared his throat, turning his attention to the silver and red garland lining the booths. "It's hard to explain," he said, eager to change the topic. "Tell me more about Chloe's K9 Creations." While in the shower, he realized why he recognized the van's logo —he'd seen those treats in Afghanistan. They'd been in a box Mom sent him only two weeks ago.

Chloe closed the menu and slipped it back behind the ketchup and mustard, drawing Belle's nose just above the table. With one warning look, and the returned strokes, she rested again. "It started out as a way to cut costs. Figured it'd be cheaper to make my own and gave me peace of mind about the ingredients. Grandma Annie taught me to sew and helped me make some dog beds and booties. Stuff like that."

"Interesting."

"No, not really. I did it to save money."

"But turned it into a business."

"That was an accident. When I find a home for a dog, I don't feel right sending them to a new home empty-handed. The dog bed, toys, and treats—all that goes with them. People tried to pay me and when I refused, they started making donations instead."

The server arrived with their plates of food. Belle's nose went into sniffing overdrive. "Behave or you'll have to get down," Parker said in a low, stern voice. Belle lifted her eyes to his, soft pants snapped shut with a lick of her lips. He waited, silent and still. She whined softly, but her head dipped back under the table to his knee.

"Ever thought about being an MP or one of those handlers your unit has with the bomb-sniffing dogs?" Chloe asked. "You're really good with her."

"Guess I've always had my sights set on Special Forces." Confused how she'd spun the topic back to him again, he took a bite of his lobster roll and nearly moaned in delight.

"Good, huh?"

Parker nodded. He wasn't sure whether the rolls were that tasty or if he was simply *that* hungry. Either way, he was happy to have four of them on his plate.

Chloe slid a treat across the table to Parker, just out of Belle's sight. "Normally, I'd suggest an entirely different kind of training approach. One that didn't include her sitting in the booth with her head on your lap waiting for something to fall, but we're improvising tonight." He stared at the bone-shaped morsel, marveling that Chloe made it herself. "Give it to her after you finish. Reward her for good behavior."

Parker raised an eyebrow at Chloe. "You know I can't adopt her," he said.

"It's a shame, but yes, I realize that."

The one thing about the military that Parker struggled with was not being able to have a dog. At first, in training and while living in the barracks, it wasn't allowed. But the higher up the ranks he climbed, the more responsibility he shouldered. With each step up, adopting a dog felt more unfair. He wouldn't be one of those owners who was never around.

But the big brown eyes staring up at him from his thigh made him wish he was on the other side of his army career so he could.

"I don't know about you, but I'm ordering dessert," Chloe announced, that sparkle in her eyes as she stared at a picture on the menu.

"It *is* Christmas, right?"

"That's the spirit! They even have holiday-themed desserts." She turned the menu and pointed. "All of these are made fresh. None of that frozen nonsense."

One glimpse at the apple pie with a scoop of ice cream and Parker was sold. He couldn't remember the last time he'd had a slice. Certainly, there wasn't an abundance of homemade pie in Afghanistan.

As the server approached their table, he felt his phone buzzing in his pocket. He considered ignoring it until after they finished, but the only people who were likely to call him were his mom or sister. "Sorry," he apologized to Chloe, holding up his phone so she could see his niece's face on the screen.

"I'll order you the apple pie. Go take the call."

He slid out of the booth, causing Belle to perk up. She looked between him and Chloe and finally slipped under the table and onto Chloe's booth.

"Uncle Parker!"

"Kaylee, when did *you* get a phone?"

His five-year-old niece giggled. "It's Mommy's phone."

"Where you guys at?" Parker expected his sister to arrive at Mom's tomorrow morning. She'd been hard-pressed to get time off work over the holidays, but his unexpected trip home certainly helped sway her boss.

"At Grandma's!" Excited yipping sounded in the background. Mom's new dog, no doubt. Parker looked over his shoulder, wondering if Chloe was the one who found Mom her companion. *It would be so easy to fall* . . . "When will you be here, Uncle Parker?" Kaylee asked, interrupting thoughts he shouldn't entertain.

"You guys are early."

"When are you coming?" Kaylee repeated, this time a little more impatiently.

"Tomorrow," Parker answered.

"Okay!" Her chipper voice warmed his chest. Kaylee was a blessing in his sister's life despite how it all came about. Parker pushed away thoughts that wouldn't do anyone any good. "Will you take me to the tree lightning cer'mony?"

35

"Of course I will," answered Parker, though he had no clue what he was agreeing to. But for his niece, he'd agree to nearly anything. This was the first Christmas he'd get to spend with her since she was two—and certainly the first one she'd remember and cherish.

"Yay!"

"Can I talk to Mommy?" he asked.

"Okay." Every word from Kaylee's mouth was filled with joy and sheer excitement. It was a refreshing contrast to the seriousness of a war zone.

"Parker, Mom says you're not going to be here until tomorrow."

"Hi, Bailey." That was his sister, always on a mission. Not one to small talk, she got right to the point. It was one of the many reasons she was such a valuable asset at her job. The reason, if Mom was on to anything, that her corporate company worked her to the bone without the pay she deserved.

"Do you want me to come get you?"

"No, don't do that." He wasn't certain whether Bailey flew to Maine or drove, but either way, he was willing to bet she'd already had a long travel itinerary herself. She needed a nap, but her inability to relax would probably forbid it.

"Are you sure? Because if you miss this tree lighting—"

"I won't."

"Better not."

"I won't—"

"Oh, geez, Kaylee's getting into the ornaments. I gotta run." Bailey ended the call before he could get in another word. Parker dropped the phone back in his cargo pocket and turned to find dessert already delivered. Chloe was appeasing Belle with another treat, though the dog's nose kept leaning sideways toward the table.

"Family?" Chloe asked as he slid back into his seat.

"My niece, Kaylee."

"Your mom mentioned you'd all be home for Christmas this year." She dove a spoon into an untouched dessert. He wasn't sure what it was, but the whipped topping was sprinkled with crushed chocolate mints. "Well, more like exclaimed it to the universe. Have I mentioned she's excited?"

Parker laughed, admiring the twinkle in Chloe's eyes a moment longer than he should. He focused on his spoon. "It's the first time since she moved to Snowy Falls that we'll all be in one place," he confirmed, eager to dig into his apple pie. He'd thought himself full earlier, but his appetite was more than accommodating for a taste of his childhood.

"Kaylee's a bright one," Chloe said. "I met her this past summer."

He waited for the questions about Kaylee's father, but when they didn't come, he let it go.

Perhaps Mom had already told Chloe the story, or maybe Chloe wasn't one to stick her nose where it didn't belong. It was . . . refreshing.

"She wants me to take her to some tree lighting ceremony," Parker said.

Chloe dabbed at her lips with a napkin that Belle was eyeing much too seriously. "The Christmas Eve tree lighting ceremony. It's an annual tradition. Has been for decades."

On instinct, Parker glanced at his watch. "Well, it's a good thing we have three whole days to make the journey home. We could walk back if it came down to it." He looked at Belle, her long tail swishing against the vinyl. "Or maybe Belle could pull us on a sled. I bet she has enough energy."

"Speaking of energy," Chloe said, dropping her spoon into her empty bowl and pushing it to the side. "We need to get Miss Belle some exercise before we go back or she might shred the comforter in the middle of the night." Her sweet tone made Belle's ears stand taller.

Parker grabbed the check when it came, ignoring Chloe's objections. "What do you have in mind?"

"There's a dog park a couple of blocks away. It has a dog run, and it's well lit." Chloe nodded toward the darkness that had fallen while they ate. He couldn't imagine having to chase down Belle in the dark if she got loose.

"How's the fence?"

"We'll want to check that," Chloe admitted. "But I think she likes us, so that helps. I've found that dogs that try to escape are usually bored and lonely. We just have to keep her motivated and her attention on us and she'll be fine. I have plenty of T-R-E-A-T-S."

Yes, it would be so easy for fall for Chloe. If only his circumstances were different. But he wasn't about to abandon a promise he made to his dad to get into the Special Forces over some whirlwind romance. Parker slipped on his coat and gloves. "Lead the way."

CHAPTER 5

HLOE

"Oh, no." Chloe tried the ignition again, but it sputtered and died as quickly as on her first attempt. What a time for her youngest brother Cole to be stuck in another county. He'd know what to do. With that option eliminated, she looked at Parker instead. "How are your mechanical skills?"

"I can change a tire," he offered with a weak laugh. "Outside of that . . ."

Chloe let out a deep breath, forcing her mind into action so it didn't have time to dwell and panic. "I can have a mechanic look at it in the morning. I bet Heidi'll know someone. But it does mean we have to walk back tonight." She glanced in her rearview at the way back to Heidi's. It wasn't that the B&B was far, only that the trek involved two very steep blocks.

"Good thing we're both wearing boots, then, isn't it?"

Chloe studied Parker a few moments longer than was probably deemed acceptable. "You're so calm," she observed. "After the trip you've had so far, how's that possible?"

Parker shrugged, clipping Belle's leash onto her collar. "Isn't the worst situation I've faced."

"Of course it's not," Chloe said, her words an apology. The shadows in his eyes hinted at much darker times he must've endured. In comparison, this inconvenience no doubt seemed like a pleasant experience. "I didn't mean—"

Parker covered her gloved hand with his own. "What do you need me to carry?"

"I can manage my bag," Chloe said, relieved for the first time on her journey back to Snowy Falls that she wasn't alone. "But if you want to grab some materials for me, I'm going to work on a new blanket for Belle tonight."

"Won't she destroy it?"

Chloe shrugged. "Probably."

By the time they were loaded up and ready to head out, Parker had almost everything on his back. How he'd created the makeshift rucksack was still a mystery to Chloe, and it left her managing only her purse and Belle. "I *can* carry more," she said.

"I don't doubt that. But why let my training go to waste?"

She lifted her hands in surrender. "When you put it like that." Chloe stared after her van, hopeful that Hollandale would remain the kind, charming town overnight. She doubted anyone would bother it—and the restaurant owner had reassured her as much—but it didn't make her feel particularly wonderful about abandoning her inventory. She'd sold out of a lot with it being Christmas, and she needed everything she had left.

"I can come back and check on it later, if you want," Parker said, already to the middle of the street while Chloe lingered on the sidewalk with Belle whining and tugging on her leash.

Chloe hurried across the street. "Thank you, but that's not necessary."

Belle leapt after Parker, snapping the leash taut and forcing Chloe to abandon her fears. *It's Christmas. The van will be fine.*

Halfway up the hill, Chloe felt the first snowflake tickle her nose. A few more yards ahead, and Belle started jumping in the air to catch puffier ones with her mouth.

"I didn't think it was supposed to snow until *after* Christmas," Parker said.

"It's not," Chloe agreed. "But if you ask

Grandma Annie, she's convinced a massive snow-storm is on its way." When Parker's smile faded, she touched his arm. It was easier to avoid those electric tingles with so many layers between them. "Don't worry. *If* she's right, we'll be back in Snowy Falls before it hits."

"I mean this with all due respect, but I hope your grandma is off her rocker about this blizzard prediction."

Chloe laughed, surprised how easily it came. Parker was nothing like she expected. Tricia bragged about a hardworking soldier who took life much too seriously. But from her experience so far, he was easygoing. He smiled far more in person than he ever did in the photos she'd seen. "I'm on your side. Most of my family'll be flying in soon, and a snowstorm doesn't bode well for them making it home in time for Christmas."

By the time they reached the top of the hill, Chloe was huffing. The orange glow of a streetlight revealed that Parker, despite all the weight on his back, looked as if he could go another dozen blocks without breaking a sweat.

Pausing to catch her breath, Belle yanked her forward via the leash. If Chloe hadn't been so distracted by Parker's silhouette, she might've been better prepared for Belle's antics, or at least held a tight grip on the leash. Instead, she squeaked as the leash slipped from her hand and she went down into a snowbank.

Belle shot off down the sidewalk.

Parker reached out a hand, but Chloe refused it. "Belle! Get Belle."

A flash of white tail caught Chloe's eye as Belle chased some critter up a tree nearly a block away. The excitable dog circled the trunk, jumping and barking every few seconds as Parker approached.

Chloe pushed herself to her feet and hurried after them, embarrassed at how easily she'd been distracted by Parker. *It can't happen again.* Belle's escape antics were not only a nuisance, but a death warrant. Chloe would never let that happen on her watch.

A loud whistle echoed down the quiet neighborhood street. Belle froze, staring at Parker. Half a second later, she charged at him as if *he* were the squirrel.

"Oh boy, here we go again."

Parker dropped to a squat, catching Belle as she slammed into him. The load on his back wobbled, but he didn't tip over. "Good girl," he said to Belle, praising her for coming back.

It's a start in the right direction. Chloe had no doubt that her previous owners had scolded Belle at every similar insistence. "You sure you don't have a dog?" She brushed the snow from the shins of her jeans. "Because you're awfully good with her."

"Grew up with dogs," Parker answered as they crossed the street, the inn coming into sight. "Yelling at her would only make her run away, right?"

"Right."

Parker handed the leash over as he held the door open. Warmth enveloped Chloe, warding off the chill of the night. The tempting aroma of snickerdoodles called to her. Belle sniffed the air, leaning into the mixed perfume of cinnamon and sugar as if she hadn't eaten anything today.

"I need to find Heidi," Chloe admitted, tightening her grip on the leash. "See about that mechanic."

"I'll take everything upstairs."

"I left the adjoining door unlocked."

Parker nodded before he took the stairs two at a time. *He must be in incredible shape.*

"Chloe, I didn't hear you guys pull up," Heidi said, appearing in a dimly lit hall.

"About that . . ."

THE LOW HUM of the TV muffled the gently howling wind outside Chloe's window. Belle wasn't a fan of the eerie noise, but she did seem appeased by the combination of occasional pats and the Christmas romance.

Chloe slipped her newly threaded needle back

into the fabric, quick stitches creating a dog bed cover she hoped the pup wouldn't destroy before they made it back to Snowy Falls. Belle watched the screen with rapture, head resting comfortably on Chloe's thigh. "Such a good girl," she murmured softly, and Belle's tail swished.

Hands occupied with the steady in and out repetition, Chloe's thoughts drifted beyond the commercial for a new fabric softener. Heidi's mechanic friend had already been called; he'd pick up the van first thing in the morning. No use worrying about what was wrong until he looked at it. Her phone battery was now one-hundred-percent dead, so touching base with either her bestie or Grandma was out of the question. If she'd thought about it, she might've asked Parker if she could borrow his, but he was passed out in the next room.

Parker. Yes, her fingers were maintaining a steady rhythm, but her mind, well, that was another matter.

More than Parker's dazzling smile or easygoing personality, he was so *good* with Belle it should be outlawed. She'd never considered finding a business partner for her rescue shelter dream, but Parker— Chloe shook away the thought, muttering when she discovered the crooked stitching her wandering mind had cost her.

"What's wrong with me, Belle? Huh?"

Belle looked up at her with those big brown eyes,

a glance capable of softening even the hardest of hearts. Moments like this, Chloe couldn't understand why anyone would give up on the pup. Sure, she had a *lot* of energy, but she was such a loveable dog. Snuggly dogs were Chloe's favorite kind.

"He's in the army," Chloe mumbled, drawing the dog's attention yet again. "For a decade or more," she repeated Parker's earlier statement. "I—" Chloe stopped when Belle lifted her head, ears perked. "What is it, girl?"

Muting the TV, Chloe listened for the sound again.

Belle hopped off the bed, whining as she trotted toward the wall. She sniffed at the baseboard, ears erect.

"Is it a mouse, or—" Then Chloe heard it, too. Groans coming from the other side of the wall. "Parker."

The dog looked back at her expectantly, as if she wanted Chloe to fix it.

Gingerly, Chloe set her sewing aside and slipped off the bed. Tiptoeing toward the wall, she leaned her ear against the green striped wallpaper and listened. The agonized moans squeezed her heart, churning the snickerdoodles she'd shared with Belle an hour ago.

Chloe'd heard more than a few stories about soldiers suffering from combat-related nightmares, but this was her first encounter with one. The last

47

thing she wanted to do was wake Parker after the miserable few days he'd had. Her gut told her he was better off with some restless sleep than no sleep at all.

"What am I supposed to do?"

Belle nudged Chloe's hand with her wet nose, adding another impatient whine before she hopped to the bathroom door.

"You want to sleep with Parker?" she asked Belle, as if the dog understood her words. Another series of groans left Belle beside herself. She clawed at the floor beneath the bathroom door. "Oh, no!" Chloe ran over and pushed the door open. Belle darted inside and slipped through the crack of Parker's adjoining door on the opposite side.

Breath frozen, Chloe waited, ready to pounce at the first hint of chaos, as Belle disappeared into the darkness of room ten.

After what felt like twenty minutes but might only have been two—she couldn't check her phone to be certain—Chloe heard nothing more than Parker's even breathing. She shouldn't peek into the room that wasn't hers, but she had to be certain Belle was nestled beside him and not secretly chewing the comforter.

A beam of moonlight revealed a peacefully sleeping soldier with his arm draped over the dog who curled against him. If Chloe didn't have a crush on Parker before, she certainly did now.

 ARKER

PARKER FELT a tickle against his wrist. Craving more sleep, he flicked his hand out, but one shake didn't get rid of the cause. "Stupid sand fly," he muttered. With a yawn, he forced his eyes open. Two large brown orbs stared back at him. Belle licked him on the chin, causing him to chuckle. "Good morning to you, too."

Her tail wagged eagerly, a textbook combat crawl bringing her even closer. Parker obliged the rubs and pats she demanded, and Belle thanked him with the occasional lick to the wrist. For such a squirrely dog who loved to shoot off like a bottle rocket given the chance, she sure did love her snuggles.

"How'd you get in here anyway?" Parker asked the dog, forcing himself to sit up in bed. The daylight of an overcast sky illuminated the room, warning him it was late morning. He hadn't slept that solid in weeks. Maybe longer.

Belle hopped off the bed and stretched, letting out an adorable yawn-moan.

Pushing away the covers, Parker grabbed his phone off the nightstand, saving the half a dozen texts from Mom for after coffee. "Nine thirty?" He shook his head, certain the late morning was due to the time change and a bit of jetlag. He hadn't slept past five since he joined the army. "Guess we better find Ms. Chloe, huh?"

Belle's tail wagged in earnest.

His knock on the opposite bathroom door was met with silence. "Chloe, are you in there?" he called and waited. When a second knock brought the same result, he assumed she was already up and moving. Maybe there was news on the van. He didn't have the heart last night to tell Mom about another delay, and decided to wait until he could tell her they were on the road this morning. Hopefully Chloe had good news.

He discovered Belle's purple braided leash curled up on the edge of the bathroom counter. "We should probably head downstairs soon. I bet there's food."

Parker changed clothes and brushed his teeth,

deciding a shave could wait one more day. It felt good, the bit of non-regulation stubble. Stuffing his wallet into a back pocket, his gaze landed on the tousled covers.

He meant to fix the bed, but the nightmare came back in chopped-up flashes before he could take a step closer.

Always the same. He couldn't even blame it on combat. No, this tormenting dream was a figment of his imagination. Irrational fear that he'd fail his squad when they needed him most. Give Dad *another* reason to decide he wasn't cut out for greatness.

A whine from Belle, who was already parked at the door, pulled him from his morbid thoughts, reminding him the best he could do was *try* to make Dad proud. He'd never hear the words, even if he succeeded. "You're right," he said to Belle, clipping on her leash and scratching behind the ears. "I shouldn't worry about any of that. It's Christmas after all."

Belle forged an eager zigzag path down the hall toward the wraparound staircase, her nose sniffing the air seconds before the aroma of bacon hit Parker.

"Good morning, you two," Chloe greeted, meeting them at the foot of the stairs. Parker's groggy vision cleared at the sight of her in dark jeans and a white sweater that sparkled the same way her eyes did. She bent over to greet Belle, leaving him to wonder what time last night the dog slipped into his room. "Come get some breakfast before it's all gone."

"I'll just take Belle out—"

"I already did." Chloe winked at him as she led him into the dining room. A couple of guests lingered in one corner, but otherwise it was empty aside from Heidi filling mugs with coffee. "I guess sleeping with you all night wasn't good enough for her, so I let her back in your room after a quick morning outing. I hope you didn't mind?"

"Not at all." Parker glanced at the husky mix, wondering if she was responsible for his mostly restful night of sleep.

"Thank you, ma'am," Parker said with a nod to Heidi when she handed him a mug.

"It's Heidi," she corrected. "Ma'am is my mother. I'll get you a plate."

Chloe stretched her neck, watching Heidi slip back into the kitchen. With the coast clear, she leaned over the table and asked in a hushed voice, "Belle didn't . . . destroy anything, did she? Comforter, sitting chair, wallpaper?"

Parker nearly spit out his coffee, choking on a sip instead. "Wallpaper?"

"I would've checked myself, but you know, not my room."

He set his cup down to prevent another mishap, looking at Belle who sat obediently at the edge of the table, tail swishing along the hardwood. "I didn't take a real close look, but I didn't notice anything alarming, if that's your concern."

"Oh, good!" Chloe let out a relieved sigh and sat back in her chair.

"Any word on the van?"

Mug lifted, Chloe's lips pinched in a tight line. "About that," she started, her mug clunking to the table a bit louder than his had.

"Here you go, Parker." Heidi slid two plates onto the table, one filled with a mountain of eggs, bacon, and some cheesy casserole, and a second, smaller one with a flaky, frosted cinnamon roll. "You came last, so I loaded you up with everything I had left."

"Thank you, Heidi. This all looks amazing." At least, there was *some* good news this morning. Because whatever Chloe had to tell him wasn't.

"I imagine it's a bit better than whatever they serve you overseas." She patted him on the shoulder before she took off for the kitchen again.

Deciding the ominous news could wait a few beats longer, he loaded up his fork. Belle stared up at him expectantly. "Persistent," he said to her. "I'll give you that." He hadn't caved at the restaurant, and he didn't plan to this morning. But the longer she bored those big brown eyes into him, the shakier his resolve became.

"I do try to train the dogs I rescue *not* to accept table scraps. I leave that spoiling up to the new owner. But Belle"—Chloe looked at him with an amused shake of her head—"she might break me."

"Do you have your own dog, or do you just foster rescues?" Parker asked, tearing apart the cinnamon roll he couldn't wait to sink his teeth into.

The glow in her eyes dimmed as she fiddled with the ceramic toothpick holder. "I haven't had my own in a couple of years. Once Bandit passed . . ." She let out a sigh. "It's hard finding a dog that gets along with other dogs. Harder to find one that'll tolerate all different kinds of dogs. Bandit, she was special."

Parker's hand covered Chloe's before he was aware he'd made the conscience decision to do so. "I'm sorry. It's hard to lose a dog."

She stared at his hand, and he wondered if she felt it too—the pulses of electricity.

"Not to spoil your meal," Chloe said, pulling her hand away and putting both in her lap, "but the van needs a new alternator."

"That doesn't sound so bad," Parker said. *Better than a failed transmission.*

"It's not bad. Easy repair. Except, the alternator *I* need doesn't exist in Hollandale. There's one on the way, but it won't get in until tomorrow morning. Parker, I'm sorry. You might've had better luck with the rental car situation."

Another day.

He pushed away the emotional worries of disappointing Mom and Kaylee—the tree lighting ceremony was still two days away after all—and focused instead on their more immediate objectives. "Are we able to stay another night?" he asked.

"Yes, Heidi said our rooms are available through New Year's. But let's hope we don't need them *that* long." Chloe shook her head. "It would be too ironic if my family made it back from Cancun in time for Christmas, but I'm stuck a few hours' drive away."

"We won't—"

"No, of course not. If we can't leave in the morning, I'll call my brother Noah. He can come pick you up and take you back to Snowy Falls."

"He's not in Cancun?"

Chloe shook her head. "No, he decided to surprise everyone for Christmas this year. He works on a remote ranch in Montana and doesn't have cell reception out there. I emailed him, but he got the news a day too late. He's staying with Grandma Annie, but if we need him, I can call on him."

Parker shouldn't care about Chloe's life or the details of it, but curiosity took over anyway. "How many siblings *do* you have?"

"There's seven of us."

"Seven?"

"I'm third in the lineup, in case you were wondering."

Parker was still trying to wrap his head around having that many siblings. Growing up, he'd only had the one younger sister. "I imagine your parents have a pretty full house at Christmas," Parker said, fishing but not willing to admit it.

"No fuller than it's been since Blakely—the youngest—was born. None of us are married yet. Well, Blakely might be. I haven't had a chance to talk to Grandma Annie and find out if they stopped the wedding. My phone died, and wouldn't you know my charger is at home?"

"You can borrow mine," Parker offered.

"Your charger won't work. My phone is ancient."

He pulled his phone from his pocket and slid it across the table. "I meant my phone. You can call your family if you need to."

"Thank you. I'll take you up on that offer this afternoon," Chloe said. "Grandma Annie's Christmas shopping all morning. She told me she was going to splurge on gifts since she took home the jackpot the other night. Then she has lunch with her ladies—" Her cheeks reddened by the second. "Sorry, you probably don't care about all that."

"You have a very intriguing family," Parker said, repocketing his phone.

Chloe fiddled again with the toothpicks. "Did you get any of your Christmas shopping done?"

Too embarrassed to admit he hadn't started, Parker shoveled another forkful of cheesy potato casserole into his mouth. He had a valid excuse—deployment—but he also had the Internet.

"I'll take that as a no," Chloe said. Before Parker

could swallow the bite he'd taken, she added, "Good thing for you, Hollandale has some wonderful shops. Why don't you finish up with your breakfast? I'll grab Belle some booties and meet you two at the stairs. She'll need some exercise before we shop. That should keep her from munching on the merchandise."

Chloe hurried out of the room before Parker could object. Though he didn't care for shopping, he wasn't upset about the prospect of spending more time with her. His commander's once-boisterous advice to avoid romantic complications was growing fainter with each passing hour he spent with Chloe.

"Is that a good thing? Or bad?" he murmured into his napkin.

CHAPTER 7

HLOE

"I'm going to need your help," Chloe said to Parker, taking a seat on the bottom stair. She peeled the Velcro open on the first of four fleece dog booties, pausing to gauge the dog's reaction. The noise intrigued Belle, but only for a moment. The squeak of the oven door in the kitchen swiveled her ears in the opposite direction, muzzle lifted to inhale the aroma of freshly baked cookies. "Hmm," Chloe mused, still on the fence about how this might go. "I have a feeling our notorious escape artist won't dig these."

Parker leaned against the doorjamb, arms folded and a dangerous gleam in his eyes. Only dangerous because Chloe was having enough trouble shoving down feelings that seemed to have sprouted overnight. This silly crush was already getting *way* out of hand.

"Belle, come here." Chloe considered clipping on her leash, but feared the restraint might make the pup fight the booties more. She didn't want to risk losing the trust she'd gained. Belle's file had very little about her time with her previous owners, excepting a laundry list of complaints. It was usually the case with a new dog, and enough of a reason to tread carefully. "I'll give you a treat if—"

Belle instantly abandoned her sniffing and pounced at Chloe's feet, ears perked and eyes alert.

"Maybe it'll be easier than you think," Parker said with a smirk.

"She is *very* motivated by rewards," Chloe surmised, breaking off the corner of a peanut butter biscuit. "But just wait. The show hasn't started yet."

Parker chuckled. "This ought to be good."

"Belle, can you shake?" The dog tilted her head in confusion, stabbing her nose in the air toward the treat Chloe harbored in her palm. "Hmm, guess you don't know that command." Gently, Chloe reached for her paw. She managed a shake and a half before Belle wriggled her leg free and whined.

Chloe felt Parker's gaze, watching too intently. Never before had she been nervous when working with a dog, no matter who was watching. But now, her pulse doubled and her fingers threatened a light tremble. *This is ridiculous, Chloe. Get a grip!* So they had one more day together. The moment they were back in Snowy Falls, they'd be consumed with their individual families. It was entirely possible the two wouldn't see each other except in passing before Parker returned overseas. Falling for this soldier wouldn't do anything but break her heart.

"Let's try this again," Chloe said to the dog, shaking away irrational thoughts that wouldn't serve her. "Sit." Belle plopped down so hard her butt shifted the runner rug back until it caught on Parker's boot. "Good girl." She gave up the treat in her hand and broke off another piece. "Now, shake." Chloe held out her treat-less palm.

Belle looked at Chloe, then the hand, and back. Seconds later, she lifted her paw and dropped it into Chloe's palm.

"Would you look at that," Parker said, admiration in his voice. Or maybe Chloe imagined that part. "Belle's a secret genius."

Chloe rewarded the dog with a second treat. "The escape artists tend to be fairly intelligent. At least that's what I've found in my limited experience."

"How long *have* you been doing this?" Parker asked as Chloe prepared another piece of bribery, hoping to slip on a bootie this time around. "Rescuing dogs?"

"Since I was a teenager, I guess. I was always taking in the strays. At least, the ones my parents would allow." She nodded toward the doorway. "Get ready to block the exit."

"You're really good with her."

Chloe glanced up at Parker, realizing the second their gazes met that she'd made a mistake. Maybe it was because she'd spent the last couple of years focused on her business instead of entertaining dates, or because she'd encountered a dog-loving soldier—an irresistible combination. Whatever the reason, she had to be careful when it came to Parker Anderson or her heart might pay the price.

"I could say the same about you." She turned her attention back to the dog. "Shake," she said to Belle. "Good girl." She slipped a bootie over her paw and Velcroed it tight before Belle could pull away. The husky shot off, running on three legs as if her leg were broken, shaking her paw in midair with every few steps.

"Dramatic much?" Parker said with a laugh, pushing off the wall to help corral Belle.

Chloe readied a second bootie and dove for a back leg when Belle leaned up against Parker's legs. "I know these are weird, Belle," Chloe said. "But it's way too cold out there for you to go without. We're going to be out there for a while."

Belle hobbled on alternating bootie-clad legs,

whining and looking up at Parker with those pitiful brown eyes.

"You poor tortured thing," Parker said, kneeling. "What is she doing to you?"

"Whose side are you on?" Chloe asked, propped on her knees and hands on her hips.

Parker cupped the dog's face with both hands and rested his forehead against Belle's. "Why, hers of course." The pup licked him on the cheek, melting Chloe's heart a little more. At this rate, she'd have a puddle of goo in her chest before the day was finished. "Are you going to take advantage of this opportunity?" Parker asked her, using that soothing dog voice as he maintained eye contact with Belle.

Chloe knelt, hiding reddened cheeks with her curls, and scooped on another bootie with lightning speed. "Three down, one to go."

Belle hobbled away, no doubt feeling betrayed.

"It's almost over," Chloe told the dog. "And there're more treats in it for you."

With perked ears, Belle awkwardly trotted toward Chloe, slipping on the hardwood planks until she reached the rug.

"One treat for one more bootie," Chloe said, holding out the bribe and looking Belle right in the eyes. "Fair trade?"

Belle plopped down without the command. Much to Chloe's surprise, she lifted the remaining paw in offering. Parker was right about the husky mix; she was incredibly intelligent. Something Chloe would have to watch carefully.

"Success!" Chloe said in palpable relief as she handed over a treat. "Let's get out the door so she doesn't try to chew through these. Once we're outside, she'll hopefully forget she has them on."

Parker shrugged into his coat as Belle sniffed beneath the front door. "We make a great team, huh?"

"We do, don't we?" It didn't seem to matter that Parker wouldn't stay. That only a few days after he was home, he'd return to his army responsibilities. Chloe still pictured the two of them together, rescuing and rehabilitating dogs. *Maybe keeping Belle.* What had Tricia called it?

Christmas magic.

"Lead the way."

DOWNTOWN HOLLANDALE WAS ONLY a block from where they enjoyed dinner the previous night, sandwiched between the restaurant and a dog park with a fenced-in run. Though the air held a crisp chill to it, the wind hadn't picked up. As long as they stayed on the move, Chloe wasn't concerned about freezing. Parker seemed even less affected by the frigid temperatures, which only made Chloe wonder more about his time in service.

"You said something about Special Forces,

right?" she asked a block from the inn, once she was certain Belle would leave her booties alone.

"Yeah."

"You *are* or—"

"Will be," Parker interrupted with an answer, his expression turning much too serious for this chilly but cheerful day. Every streetlight in Hollandale was decorated with a giant wreath and massive red bow. Snowmen lined the front yards of the houses they passed. Chloe regretted the prodding that took away from the ambiance. But she was too curious to leave it alone.

"After the deployment?" she guessed.

"Yeah."

Back to short answers. Chloe recognized his shift in mood for what it was—a warning to stop pressing. What she didn't understand, however, was *why* he wouldn't want to talk about something he was so passionate about. She left the topic for another time and instead asked, "Do you have any ideas about gifts?"

"Yeah," Parker said, scrubbing a gloved hand along the back of his neck. "Gifts aren't exactly my strong point."

A challenge. "Good thing you have me, then."

She felt his gaze on her as they crossed a residential street and descended the steep hill. The uneasiness of moments ago faded. "Yeah, it is," Parker said, sending irrational tingles throughout Chloe. It was easy enough to blame the cold. Harder to unravel and face their true source.

"Your mom is easy," Chloe said as the dog park came into sight. Three other dogs raced inside the fenced-in area, already causing Belle's ears to perk. There were no notes in her file to indicate she didn't get along with other dogs. "She loves snowmen. Has them up all year round."

"Are you besties with my mom?" Parker teased.

"She's been my neighbor for three years. Friendships are a hazard of small-town living, in case you didn't know that."

"Kind of forgot that's how it works."

"How long do you get to stay?" Chloe dared to ask. "Before you have to go back to Afghanistan. It *is* Afghanistan, right?"

"Yeah," he answered. "I have to fly out just after New Year's."

Chloe shouldn't have asked. Maybe then her heart wouldn't have soared that little bit with hope. A few extra days didn't mean anything could come of this. Whatever *this* even was. "What does your niece like?" she asked, refocusing her thoughts on gifts as she unlocked the first of two gates into the dog park.

"Kaylee is easy," Parker said. "That girl is obsessed with Snoopy. It's all she talks about on our calls. If you ever need to rehome a beagle, my sister *will* kill you. But you'd be Kaylee's hero for life."

Chloe kept Belle on the leash as a golden retriever trotted over. Both tails wagged as they sniffed and said hello. "You want to play, Belle?" Chloe asked softly, freeing the dog from her restraint. Belle and her new friend raced across the snow-covered area, no warning signs to be had. "Where does your sister live?"

"You're not seriously considering the beagle—"

Chloe laughed. "No, I'm not trying to make enemies with your family."

"Bailey lives in North Carolina."

With Belle enjoying the company of her new friend, Chloe found a bench and sat down. "I always thought I'd travel more with this . . . I don't know what you call it. It's not exactly a job."

"Calling?" Parker offered, sitting next to her. She tried to ignore the heat she felt from his nearby leg, blaming the small bench for the close proximity that was messing with her thoughts.

"I guess you could call it that." Chloe dug around in her purse for the mint lip balm she knew was in there somewhere. "I've rescued dogs from all over. But most of the dogs from any distance away come on a plane." She handed him a tennis ball that seemed to keep popping to the top of her purse, and finally secured the lip balm. "Belle isn't the only interesting airport pickup I've experienced."

"I suspect she's the most exciting, though."

Chloe laughed, the butterflies in her stomach settling to a gentle flutter. "I think she wins that award for sure." She swiped the nearly frozen lip balm across her lips, catching how his gaze tracked her gesture then settled, for just a moment, on her mouth. The butterflies nearly had a heart attack en masse.

Belle raced up to them, the golden at her side. Both dogs eagerly greeted them, demanding neck rubs.

"Gracie," a woman about Chloe's age called after the golden. "I'm sorry, is she bothering you?"

"Not at all," Parker said before Chloe could, his words making her forget which station her train of thought had just pulled into. *If only he lived in Snowy Falls.* "This is Belle."

"She's a beautiful dog. What breed?"

"Husky-shepherd mix is all I know for sure. I'd bet she has a trace of lab in there too."

"Are you two new to town?"

"Oh, no," Chloe answered automatically. "Just passing through. Parker was lucky enough to snag some leave over the holidays."

"Military?" the woman guessed, a little too much interest in her eyes for Chloe's liking.

"Army," Parker answered.

"He's home from a deployment, actually."

Understanding seemed to flash through the woman's eyes. "Thank you for your service. I hope you two have a lovely Christmas together. You're both very brave."

Chloe's eyebrow arched at that, but the woman slipped out with Gracie before she could question it. Parker smiled, apparently understanding where Chloe did not. "She thinks we're together," he said.

"What?"

"Married."

You're both very brave. "Oh. Oh! Sorry, I didn't mean—"

Parker laughed, patting at her knee before he rose from the bench. "You're cute when you're flustered, did you know that?"

Cute? Chloe felt a blush assault her cheeks and hoped she could blame the cold for the bright red color she was no doubt sporting. *Did he really just call me cute?*

"I wonder if Belle knows how to play fetch." Parker tossed the tennis ball she'd given him into the air a couple of times, seemingly oblivious to the effect of his words.

CHAPTER 8

ARKER

"Thanks for letting me use your phone," Chloe said, weaving her way into the corner of their second stop. Scarves and wall hangings filled the walls of the gift shop, and Parker wasn't sure how he was supposed to know what any of the women in his life would like. He'd been absently browsing with Belle on a short leash while he waited for Chloe to call her grandma, but was still uncertain if anything in this corner would make a nice gift. *I just don't have a knack for this.*

Chloe handed over his phone, and Belle lifted her nose to the exchanged device. Parker chuckled, letting her get in a good, albeit disappointing, sniff.

"You're welcome to use it again." He longed to ask how everything was on the home front, but refrained. The more invested he became with Chloe's life, the harder it'd be to leave. The harder it'd be to remain unattached. He could so easily fall for Chloe Taggert, if only he let himself. *I can't let that happen.*

"Grandma Annie's still convinced we'll be buried in ten feet of snow come morning."

The warning, however nonchalant, prodded Parker to check the weather forecast on his phone. Snowflakes were expected to start in the middle of the night, but nothing on the app drew concern for an all-out blizzard. "She ever right about these things?" Parker asked, a sliver of worry slipping past his defenses as he put away his phone and browsed the shelves.

"About fifty-fifty, I'd say."

"You don't seem worried."

Chloe gave an indifferent shrug. "Not much we can do to change the weather, right?"

"Right."

The scent of lavender drifted to him as Chloe took a step closer, placing her hand on his arm. "I'm going to do everything in my power to get you home in time for Christmas. This ride's had a few more detours than we planned, but Kaylee *will* get to attend the Christmas Eve tree lighting ceremony with her uncle. You have my word."

A blonde curl caught in Chloe's white knit scarf. Parker hooked a finger through the strand and set it free. He blamed the cramped store for their proximity. Otherwise he'd take a step back and put a safer distance between them. *Or would I?* "Thank you, Chloe."

"For what?" He caught her eyes drop to his lips and flicker away. It set his pulse racing.

"You didn't have to help me out at all. The delays —whatever they may be—aren't your fault."

He could kiss her. It'd be so easy. Just tuck one finger beneath her chin and tilt her lips toward his. The shiny layer of lip gloss made him wonder what flavor he'd taste. One kiss wouldn't change the course of his future or unravel all his plans. *Right?*

"Belle!" With wide eyes, Chloe lunged for the dog. The fringes of a checkered blue and white scarf hung from her mouth. She squatted down, firmly but gently scolding Belle until she relinquished her pilfered prize. "Never a dull moment with this one, huh?"

"I'll buy that," Parker offered, nodding at the scarf.

Chloe shook her head. "I should've been watching her. I'll buy it. After a wash, I can give it to Libby. Blue's her favorite color. I'll just have to do it in secret so none of my other siblings feel gypped with just one gift instead of two."

"You buy gifts for *all* of them?" Parker asked.

"Of course. It's not their fault our parents decided to have a gaggle of kids." She held on to Belle's collar, keeping the dog against her leg until they reached the front counter.

Parker followed, still astounded, not only by Chloe's generosity, but by her family. He still couldn't picture having six brothers and sisters. With the rapturous way Chloe talked about her family, he wished he could have a taste of it for himself. Growing up in her house had to be drastically different than his much quieter childhood.

"I think the store next door will have just what your mom needs," Chloe said over her shoulder as she handed the cashier her card. "I have a good feeling about it." Belle nudged demandingly at her hand until Chloe stroked her head. "Then yes, we will find lunch. You can't live on T-R-E-A-T-S all day."

"Can't say I blame her," the elderly man behind the register said. The light glared against his glasses as he lifted his head and fixed his gaze on Parker. "We sell out of those treats two days after she drops off a fresh shipment. I can't keep any of her stuff in stock."

Parker admired Chloe's display on the counter, wondering how many other stores in Maine carried her homemade treats. He'd no doubt that Chloe's K9 Creations could be an empire, if only she wanted it to be. "They're very good, if Belle has anything to say about it."

"Got any more of those tug-of-war ropes?" the man asked Chloe. "Lots of folks been asking about those."

"Fresh out, I'm afraid. I'll make sure to bring some on my next trip. Lane promised to bring me some rope. I'll remind him." Chloe lifted a pair of earrings from a jewelry rack on the counter, a smile curling the edges of her lips as she admired them. The twinkle in her eyes made Parker forget all about this Lane character she mentioned, maybe a brother, maybe more.

"Who would that be for?" Parker asked over her shoulder, studying the crystal rhinestone earrings in the shape of snowflakes.

"What?"

"Which sister? Or maybe for your grandma?"

"Not quite Grandma Annie's style. Blakely's the only one who wears earrings besides me, but she's way too picky to shop for." Chloe abandoned the earrings as she accepted her card and stuffed it in her purse. "I just thought they looked nice."

Parker followed her to the door and waited until they were outside. "*You* want them."

"I don't need them."

"You don't buy gifts for yourself very often, do you?"

"They're an indulgence I don't need. I wouldn't even have a place to wear them. Dangly earrings and rambunctious dogs aren't exactly a winning combination. Besides, the money could be spent on better things." She sent him a smile, but he noticed a dimness in her eyes that spoke of something more. "C'mon," she said, tugging on his arm and pulling him into the next store. "I think I see a display of snowmen."

If Parker questioned his feelings about Chloe before, he was less able to deny them now. The money she refused to spend on the earrings would no doubt go toward Belle or whichever dog she took in next. Her selfless nature and generous heart, those were qualities he wanted in a— *Knock it off, Parker. This can't work. Focus.*

"What do you think?" Chloe nodded at a bookcase display filled with an assortment of snowmen. From salt and pepper shakers to end table decorations to framed art, the shelf offered all varieties. "Anything speak to you?"

"I thought you were helping me," he countered.

"I did. I led you here. But the gift has to come from you. Besides, your mom will know if I picked it out."

He pretended to scan the assortment, but really he was stealing side glances at Chloe. He wondered how close she'd become with Mom. He wondered more why it mattered to him.

"Parker?"

"What about this one?" He reached for the first snowman his eyes landed on—a beautiful glitter-covered disaster. He regretted his wandering thoughts when he spotted the sparkly pile it left on the shelf. "Maybe *not* this one."

Chloe laughed as silver glitter erupted when he set it back down. "You, uh, have glitter on your—" She pointed to her own cheek, giggling more when Parker failed to wipe it away.

A look in the snowman-shaped mirror revealed he'd only made matters worse. "There's glitter caught in my stubble."

"At least it's festive," Chloe teased, digging in her purse. She ripped open a packet and held out a wet towelette. "Here, let me get it."

"That'll work?" he asked, leery of furthering the glitter spread.

"My best friend is a librarian at an elementary school. She swears by these after any kind of art project." Chloe rubbed the damp cloth against his cheek, the graze of her delicate fingers reigniting the urge he'd just tamped down to kiss her. "Got it."

Parker leaned toward the mirror, shaking away the irrational urges. "That's better."

"Easier to clean you up than Belle," Chloe said.

Glancing down at the dog, the shimmer of glitter sparkled in a dozen places from the top of her head to the tips of her ears. The dog's expression, oblivious to glitter troubles and hopeful for fingers combing behind her ears, made Parker burst out in laughter. "Maybe the wind'll take care of that on the walk home."

"Attempt number two," Chloe instructed. "Try something that doesn't shed as much."

Parker scanned the shelf, determined to concentrate this time. These wandering thoughts were what his commander had warned him against. He promised they'd make the training near impossible to pass. *They'll be worse if it's a new thing.*

"What about this one?" Parker pointed to a vintage metal snowman, a present dangling from one branch hand and a star from the other. He thought Mom would appreciate the green scarf and the rustic design. He could see it hanging on the wall, maybe near the entrance or in the kitchen.

"I think it's perfect," Chloe said.

"You do?"

"Yes, I do." The dazzling approval in her eyes set his pulse to double-time again.

Distance. They needed distance or things would get carried away. The attraction between them was undeniable, and he'd bet his return trip that she felt it, too. But it couldn't lead anywhere. Once they were back at the inn, he'd hole up in his room. Put his head in his training manuals and focus on preparing for his future.

Except.

Future.

The simple word sounded hollow against his inner ear. It wasn't a goal, or a deadline. It felt . . . *lonely*.

"One down," he said, wishing he was finished as badly as he wished he had a dozen siblings to shop for.

"Your sister's the challenge," Chloe said. "Can I borrow your phone?"

He handed it over without forethought.

"Hmm, you don't have Facebook."

"Used to," he admitted.

"Let me guess. Military thing?"

"Yeah." He wouldn't be allowed to have social media accounts soon enough, or so he'd been told. He cut ties before the deployment so it wouldn't fester into a problem later. Mom wasn't particularly happy about his decision, but she understood as long as he still sent pictures when he could. Social media wasn't a threat Dad had faced during his military days.

"Guess we're going to have to do this the old-fashioned way. But first, lunch." She tugged at his arm, pulling him toward the front counter to pay for the snowman, leaving him to wonder what her cryptic words meant. He was getting used to her leading him around, and Parker had to admit, he didn't mind it at all.

CHAPTER 9

C HLOE

"Wow, did you two empty out the stores?" Heidi asked when Chloe closed the door behind them. Parker's arms were draped with shopping bags, making the question valid. "Look at that haul!"

"Let's just say, Parker's all set for Christmas." Chloe knelt to remove Belle's booties. With each one gone, the pup became antsier and antsier. Freed from the last one, she bolted up one staircase and down another—twice—eliciting laughter from every witness.

"She's certainly happy to have *those* off," Parker said, lingering at the foot of the stairs. Chloe couldn't decide if he was waiting to be dismissed, or wondering what came next. Either way, she wasn't ready to go their separate ways. The thought of turning in and not seeing him until morning made her feel robbed of time that wasn't even hers to covet. The yearning continued just the same.

"I made some pumpkin soup," Heidi announced when Belle finally slowed and trotted over to her for head scratches. "Should be ready within the hour."

"It already smells divine," Chloe said, shedding her coat and draping it over an arm. The savory, pumpkin aroma, mixed with a tease of homemade biscuits, reminded Chloe lunch had been several hours earlier.

"I might take a raincheck," Parker said, already two steps up and half turned away. "I have some studying to do. Mind if I steal a couple cookies and hole up in my room for the rest of the night?"

"Oh, you can't do that!" Heidi interjected. "You two should go ice skating. It's a Hollandale tradition. Since you're stuck here, you have to go. Don't you start about not having skates, either. There are rentals down at the park. They have hot chocolate, music, and my personal favorite, fresh baked muffins."

Parker stared at the red runner on the stairs, his hesitation loud as a siren to Chloe. She chimed in to save him. "Belle and ice skating don't strike me as pairing well together. Maybe another time."

"I'll watch her."

Both Chloe and Parker looked at Heidi in surprise. Belle was certainly a lovable dog, but she was mischievous and destructive when anxious. "I'd hate to come back and find out she chewed off one of your dining room chair legs," Chloe said, half-joking, half-serious.

"She'll be a good girl, won't you Belle?"

The dog looked at Chloe with those innocent brown eyes, almost as if she were begging. Her only excuse gone, Chloe looked at Parker, giving him a chance to opt out. They'd already spent the day together. Surely, he wanted some time to himself, no matter how much Chloe now wanted to go. "If you need to study—"

"I really *should* hit the books," Parker agreed, gratitude flashing in his eyes.

Any relief was undone with Heidi's stern, disapproving expression. "It's Christmas, Parker. Do you want to look back on this holiday and remember spending it with your nose in some book? Would your *mother* want to hear that's how you spent your leave?"

Chloe bit her bottom lip, hiding a smile at Parker's shamefaced reaction. "Ice skating sounds great, ma'am . . . er . . . Heidi."

"Good!" Heidi clapped her hands together. "Now that we've got that settled, I'll see you two down here for supper in an hour. You'll want to head over to the park right after, before it gets too crowded. Plus, you'll have that long drive ahead of you tomorrow. Need to make sure you get enough sleep." She added the last with a wink, making Chloe wonder if she was up to something.

"C'mon, Belle," Chloe called. "You're stuck with me until supper."

~

THOUSANDS of white Christmas lights illuminated Hollandale Memorial Park. Lights hung from the trees, along the eaves of picnic shelters, and around the ice rink. Chloe was certain she'd never seen anything closer to a true winter wonderland than the sight before them now. It was like something out of a romantic Christmas movie.

"Isn't it beautiful?" Chloe asked, unable to contain her excitement. If she had to be stranded, this wasn't a bad place for it to happen. The company wasn't half bad either. She didn't even mind her chilly fingers, the tips of each like icicles despite her gloves. "Let's get our skates!" She looped her arm through Parker's, hurrying him down the sidewalk toward the skate rental trailer.

"Have you done this before?" Parker asked as they waited in a short line.

"Ice skating?" Chloe asked.

"Yeah."

"All the time. We have a pond twice this size in

Snowy Falls, but I have to admit, their Christmas light game lacks in comparison." She scooted forward in line. "Wait, have you *not* been ice skating before?"

He shuffled from one foot to the other, hands stuffed in his coat pockets. "No." He said the word so quietly she wasn't convinced he'd spoken at all.

"Was that a—"

"No, I haven't."

"I'd say it's like riding a bike, but that wasn't my experience."

Parker lifted an eyebrow, staring at her as if he wanted her to continue. But those dang butterflies were sure active this evening.

"I crashed a lot as a kid," she said quickly, words mashed together in their haste to be out. "But rest assured, if someone as uncoordinated as I used to be can learn to skate, there's hope for everyone. And I do mean *everyone*."

"We could be inside. Where it's warm and there's a TV."

A snowflake kissed Chloe's cheek. "And miss all this? C'mon. It won't be that bad. I'll teach you. I only broke my leg once." When Parker's eyes widened, she added, "Kidding! I'm kidding. Bad joke, I know. I did twist an ankle one winter. But I was nine and someone dared me to do a spin—"

"You are something, Chloe Taggert. That's for sure."

"I hope that's a compliment." Flirting. Yes, she

was definitely flirting. She blamed the butterflies and the romantic winter ambiance.

"Very much so."

Okay, now he's *flirting.*

"What sizes?" the woman at the window asked, saving Chloe from saying something embarrassing that might shatter the moment. She was starting to *feel* things for Parker. Real things that might become a problem later.

"Promise me no broken bones," Parker said, much too serious. "My commander will kill me if I show back up to the FOB with a cast."

"What's a FOB?"

"Stands for Forward Operating Base. Basically, what we call the different bases overseas."

Skates in hand, Chloe led them to a bench. It was easy to forget that Parker was in the army when he was out of uniform. Easier still to dismiss the reality that in a few days, he'd be gone. It might be another Christmas—or three—before she saw him again.

"Where are we supposed to put our shoes?" Parker asked.

"Lockers over there," she said with a nod, slipping off her boots. The chilly air bit at her toes despite her fuzzy wool socks. "Relax, Parker. Your commander won't have any reason to curse my name. At least, I don't think he will."

Jazzy Christmas music echoed from a speaker on

a light pole as they entered the ice rink, but it seemed to do little for Parker's uneasiness. He wobbled onto the ice, one hand firmly gripping the straw bale wall.

"Buck up, soldier," Chloe said, reaching out her hand. "It's just a little ice."

He waved away her offer but let go of the twine he had a death grip on.

"Did you ever rollerblade as a kid?" Chloe asked.

"Yeah, I think so."

"Well, it's a little like that. Just no hills to worry about out here."

Parker cracked a smile, forcing himself forward with steadier legs. She had to give him credit, he was still upright halfway around the rink. He left his worried expression on the other side, increasing his pace when the music picked up, and shooting off ahead.

Surprised at how quickly he picked up something he claimed to have never tried, Chloe worked her legs to catch up, panting her accusation at him. "Are you *sure* you haven't done this before?"

"First time. I promise."

"You're not like some secret hockey star, are you?"

"No."

"What did you do? Before you joined the army?" Chloe risked the question, knowing full well he might shut down on her again. She'd met a couple similar roadblocks during lunch when she peppered him with other questions. Happy to answer anything about his sister, so they could figure out her gift, he'd dodged anything remotely personal like bullets.

"The usual. College. Desk job."

Chloe turned her head and stared at him. "*You* worked a desk job?"

"Is that so hard to believe?"

"It's just, well, it's the opposite of what you do now."

"Not really. It's not as action-packed and glamorous as you think. I spend a lot of time on a computer analyzing data; studying maps."

Though half a dozen questions instantly emerged, Chloe bit her tongue. It was the most he'd told her about his military life, and she didn't want to discourage him. Maybe, if she were quiet, he'd open up a little more.

"I joined the army when my dad got sick. He lived to see me graduate basic training, but not long after that."

"I'm so sorry, Parker." Chloe automatically reached for his hand. Despite her rash gesture, Parker held on as they skated.

With each easy lap, more families poured onto the ice, and after a lap of silence, Parker finally added, "He's been gone six years now."

"I can't imagine losing my dad," Chloe said, sadness clenching her chest for his loss. A loss she swore she could feel as if it were her own. She glanced at their connected hands, wondering if she was imagining all this. "I'm sure he's very proud of you."

Parker huffed a laugh that suggested otherwise, pulling his hand away. "Maybe he'll be, once I become a Green Beret."

"Special Forces?" Chloe guessed, choosing each word delicately now. Fearing the wrong one could cause him to clam up again, maybe for good this time.

"Yeah."

The music overhead transitioned from upbeat and lively to slow and romantic. Chloe didn't recognize the tune, but couples all over the rink joined hands. She wished she hadn't shattered their moment. Maybe they'd be one of those couples now if she hadn't.

"I hope Belle's not chewing on a curtain while Heidi's passed out in her chair," Chloe said, hoping to lighten the mood. Thankfully, it worked.

"Should've made her sign a liability waiver," Parker teased.

Chloe kept staring at his hand, wishing she could take it again. Wishing— *What do I wish?*

"Chloe, look out!" Parker yanked her toward him so quickly she didn't have time to set her feet.

The two went down in a hard tumble, Parker harder since he cushioned most of her fall. A kid, no more than six or seven, whisked by. Chloe had been so distracted she nearly plowed over a child. *Oh, geez.*

"You okay?" She lifted her cheek off Parker's chest, meeting his eyes. Praying she hadn't smashed the soldier to smithereens. It wasn't a wince of pain or trickle of blood she found, though, but an enormous grin. With her fears put to rest, Chloe realized how close her lips were to his. She could just lean in . . . the last few inches . . . and kiss him. *Oh*, how she wanted to kiss him.

"You nearly ran over a kid," Parker said with a hearty laugh.

She could blame her sudden, heated blush on the cold, but she couldn't hide it this close to him. "I got distracted. Are you okay? No broken bones?"

"Distracted by what?"

"You." The word slipped out before she could stop it. Her heart thrummed in her chest, butterflies going mad in her stomach. "I mean—"

Parker reached his hand up to her cheek, meeting her halfway. His lips pressed against hers, and in that moment everything else disappeared. She didn't hear the laughter of children, the Christmas music, or even the scrape of skates on ice. She only heard her wildly beating heart. Her fingertips tingled to life, no longer cold. The ice beneath them felt more like a cloud, soaring high in the sky.

Everything she desired and feared was true: she was falling *hard* for Parker Anderson.

CHAPTER 10

ARKER

I⟨T wasn't⟩ repetitive nightmares that kept Parker awake his second night at the inn. It was the remembrance of Chloe's kiss on his lips. The sound of her sweet laughter that filled the rest of the evening embedded in his memory. Her bold, spunky personality making him smile. They skated until their shins burned.

He was up before the sun, but he didn't feel restless or tired. He felt . . . rejuvenated.

And only a little lonely. A glance at the barely cracked bathroom door didn't reveal a furry nose snuffling his way. His room felt surprisingly empty without the rambunctious husky. *Must've known Chloe needed you more last night.*

"Now I'm talking to a dog that isn't here." He chuckled, scrubbing a hand over his stubble and searching the room for a distraction.

Half a dozen gift bags sat piled in a sitting chair. He could ask Chloe to help him wrap his gifts. *All except one.*

Parker reached into the largest bag and pulled out the little bag he'd stashed. He'd been feigning a phone call while Chloe waited on dessert and gone back for the snowflake earrings right after they finished eating. With the store next door to the restaurant, it felt like a sign.

In fact, most things the past couple of days felt like signs.

The earrings twinkled in the early morning light. *We can make this work, right?*

He hid the small bag in a dresser drawer for safekeeping, debating when to give them to Chloe. Should he give them to her tonight so she could wear them over the holidays, or save them for the traditional day?

With a yawn, he decided coffee should come before any major decisions. He showered, shaved, and headed downstairs for breakfast with a cheeky grin spread across his lips. Any advice from his commander was but a faint whisper. He couldn't control the way he felt about Chloe any more than he could control the weather.

Maybe he should embrace this unexpected event for what it was: a blessing. Or as his mom would call it this time of year: *Christmas magic*.

"Good morning, Heidi," Parker greeted warmly, discreetly sniffing the air for a hint of breakfast but coming up empty. Aside from the faint trace of cinnamon, he didn't smell anything. He hoped there was coffee.

Heidi spun from the table she was wiping down, her usual chipper smile missing and a frazzled expression in its place. "Morning, Parker. I'm sorry about breakfast. It's going to be late this morning. If we keep the power."

"Power?" Cautiously, Parker approached a window and parted the curtain. A solid sheet of white covered two-thirds of the glass. He'd need a step stool to see over the top of it. *A drift?*

"Snowstorm hit overnight. Can you believe that? Not a word about more than an inch or two in the forecast, yet half the town is out of power. The wind'll knock it out here soon enough."

Dread filled Parker as he realized Chloe's grand-ma's prediction came true. Christmas Eve was tomorrow. The last thing he wanted to do was break Kaylee's heart by missing the tree lighting ceremony. Better to stay busy than stew. "What do you need done?"

"You're a guest, Parker. I couldn't ask you—"

"I'm offering." He moved to another window, one without a drift taller than he was. The few cars in the lot were covered in snow, recognizable only by the mounds of snow. "Do you have a shovel?"

"I'll do you one better. I have a snowblower."

Good. With this wind, Parker could spend all day outside with a shovel and never finish. "Let me grab my coat and gloves."

"Thank you, Parker. That's more than generous of you. My maintenance guy is out of town until after Christmas. We weren't supposed to get any snow. A neighbor down the block might come through with his Bobcat later, but no guarantees, you know."

He took the stairs two at a time, nearly colliding with Chloe as he turned the corner. Time seemed to stop as his gaze took her in. Her golden curls, the dimple he'd only noticed last night while he was laid out on the ice rink, and her soft hunter green sweater all combined to steal his breath. It'd be so easy to reach out and slip an arm around her waist.

"In a hurry?"

Belle forced her head beneath his hand, wedging herself between them until she could lean against his legs. "I bet you'd like to play in the snow, huh?"

"Snow?" Chloe asked, eyebrows drawn.

"You haven't looked outside?"

"No." She looked over her shoulder, toward the window at the end of the hall. "Do I want to?"

"Let's just say, next time your grandma makes a crazy weather prediction, I'm placing a sizable bet. On *her*."

"It's bad, isn't it?" Her expression wasn't concerned as much as guilty. "I knew I should've had the van serviced before I left for Bangor. I just ran out of time. If I had, maybe we wouldn't be stuck here, *again*. Parker—"

He took her into his arms, cupping her cheek. "Being stuck here hasn't been all *that* bad, Chloe." He placed a gentle kiss on her lips. One kiss turned into two. The howling wind and whine from Belle interrupted the third, reminding him a task waited outside.

"Good morning to you, too," Chloe said, a goofy grin on her face.

Parker traced her cheek with his knuckles. "I'm going to clear the drive."

"We'll help. Well, *I'll* help. Belle will probably just play in the snow." Belle wagged her tail at the mention of her name. "I'll grab her booties and meet you downstairs."

"Maybe you should look outside before you commit." He felt as if he were floating on a cloud. He didn't know how this could work, or even if it would. Really, the odds against them were stacked higher than some of the drifts outside. But he wanted to try.

He collected his phone from the nightstand, not surprised to see three missed calls and a string of texts. He dialed Mom's number just as another text came through.

"Parker, you're okay! Please tell me you haven't gotten on the road this morning."

"No, we're snowed in."

"Oh, good."

Parker chuckled. "Not the reaction I was expecting."

"There've been a couple of terrible accidents on the highways this morning. I'm just— Well, it's no matter. You're both safe and sound." He waited as Mom rambled about the snow accumulation, road closures, and the town scrambling to pull off the tree lighting. "Kaylee will be devastated if they cancel."

"They won't." Parker wasn't sure how he knew, but he felt certain.

"Christmas magic," Mom agreed. "You're right."

"Still singing that old tune?" he teased.

"Parker James Anderson, Christmas magic is real and alive. You just need a little faith."

He almost told her he already knew she was right, but that'd only get Mom worked up and excited. It was too soon for all that. "We're going to get the drive cleared," he said. "I have to meet Chloe downstairs. She's waiting."

"How *is* Chloe?"

"Good." Parker scrubbed a hand over the back of

his neck, warring between asking her for advice and staying quiet. She'd endured Dad's time in the Special Forces. Maybe she'd have something useful to offer from a woman's perspective. Reassurance that a new relationship could survive the rigorous training schedule. The rest . . . he'd figure that out. "I didn't know you two were attached at the hip, though," he said instead, teasing.

"You really need to spend more time in Snowy Falls. Remember what it's like to live in a small town. I bet it'd do you good."

"Mom," he warned.

"I know, I know. You're career Army. Can't blame me for wanting my son nearby."

The silence spoke of what they knew, but refused to acknowledge, aloud. Ever since Dad had gotten sick, and Parker'd enlisted, visits home were scarce. Once he started his training, anything like scheduled leave would be a phantom. He could be called away at any hour of the day or night. For the first time, his commitment made him pause. *Is this really what I want?* "I better go before they get started without me."

"Parker?"

"Yeah, Mom?"

"Chloe's special. You've probably figured that out for yourself, but I had to say it."

"Yeah, I have. Gotta run, Mom. I'll call later with another update." He ended the call before Mom could get carried away. Everything was happening so fast. He only met Chloe three days ago. Nothing in his life had ever worked that fast before. *But it feels right*. He wanted to make it work with Chloe, but it was too soon to know if he could.

CHAPTER 11

HLOE

"Looks like you have reinforcements out there," Chloe said to Heidi, unwinding her scarf and draping it on a coat hook as Belle charged inside, slipping and sliding on the hardwood. Half an hour after she and Parker cleared the sidewalks, driveway, and cars, a Bobcat rolled up to offer assistance. Chloe had to admit it felt slightly hopeless before help arrived.

"Ah, that'll be Brad." Heidi set up a few coffee mugs next to the brewing pot. "He lives down the street."

"I just love small towns, don't you?" She rubbed her hands together to ward off the chill.

"I couldn't imagine living anywhere else."

Chloe noticed a couple of guests sitting in the dining room, sipping on coffee. Heidi's usual pastry plate was missing from the coffee table. "Do you need help in the kitchen?" she offered.

"You two are spoiling me," Heidi said with a smile and shake of her head. "But yes, if you're free, I'd love the help. Breakfast is in the oven finally, but it's lunch I'm worried about. And the cookies. I'm clean out and can't imagine Christmas Eve without snickerdoodles. I wasn't raised that way."

After Belle was freed from her booties, Chloe slipped a treat from her pocket. "Can you behave in the kitchen or you going to cause problems?" she asked the dog before handing over the morsel.

"Belle will be an angel, won't you?" Heidi chimed in. The husky's tail swished along the floor in agreement.

Heidi put Chloe to work on the cookies so she could start a pot of soup for lunch. It reminded Chloe of Christmas Eve two years ago when she was volunteered to help Grandma Annie prepare the holiday feast. Admittedly, a simple batch of cookies was nothing in comparison to the dozen side dishes she'd been responsible for that year.

Chloe smiled to herself as she measured the cream of tartar. Noah's surprise visit had likely earned him that spot in Grandma's kitchen this year. It made Chloe wonder if her family'd made it home from Cancun yet. Had Blakley eloped, or did they save her from the hot-shot city lawyer who'd no doubt break her heart? All the tiny details she might know if she had a phone charger. Later, she'd ask to use Parker's phone again.

What would Christmas be like this year? *If we make it home.* "What are you doing for Christmas, Heidi?"

"The usual," she said with a shrug, chopping celery stalks and scooping handfuls into a stockpot.

Chloe remembered Heidi's husband had passed away several years before. They didn't have kids, and she never remarried. She hoped Heidi wasn't planning to spend the holidays alone.

Heidi caught Chloe watching her and offered a smile. "I'll still have four guests after you two get on the road. They'll be cleared to drive on by morning, you'll see."

Chloe nodded, paying attention to the eggs as she cracked them into a bowl. "Do you have any Christmas Eve traditions?"

"I have a pot roast for tomorrow night. Plus, we usually sing Christmas carols and play a few games. Then I do a huge breakfast spread on Christmas morning before church."

"Sounds wonderful," Chloe said, and meant it. "I almost wish we could stay, but Grandma Annie would never forgive me for missing Christmas Eve dinner. And Parker's niece will be disappointed if he doesn't make it to Snowy Falls in time for the tree lighting tomorrow."

Heidi looked up from her cutting board. "You two seem to get along well."

Chloe couldn't fight the smile that spread on her lips. The memory of their kiss last night *still* made her tingly and warm. Not to mention the stolen kisses from this morning. "Parker's nice. He's so good with Belle." The dog perked at the mention of her name, no doubt hoping for a handout. She was behaving better than Chloe expected; no doubt, the exercise in the snow earlier had worn her out. "I wish he could adopt her. They'd be such a perfect pair together."

"Why don't *you* adopt Belle?" Heidi suggested, dropping an array of chopped vegetables into the pot.

"Me?"

"Why not?" Heidi challenged. "You're just as good with her as he is. And who knows. Someday, Belle might belong to both of you."

"Oh, I don't know about that."

"Really?"

Chloe hid a guilty smile as she measured sugar into a mixing bowl. "He's in the army. That adds . . . complications."

"It does," Heidi agreed. "But imagine how many more dogs you could help if you were in other locations. You'd get to travel, like you've always talked about doing." Heidi chopped through a few carrots with lightning speed. "You might miss your family, though."

"And Snowy Falls." Chloe loved her hometown, and never imagined *living* anywhere else. Most of her siblings were only a phone call and a few blocks away. Yes, she wanted to travel. But Maine was home base in all those scenarios she'd dreamed up. Moving around every few years would also make it harder to set up a rescue facility. *But how else does this work?*

"Do you love him?" Heidi's abrupt question caused Chloe to drop a teaspoon filled with vanilla extract into the bowl.

"I just met him."

"You don't believe in a little Christmas magic?"

Belle hopped to her feet half a second before Parker emerged into the kitchen. "You're officially unburied," he announced. His gaze fell on Chloe, warming her chest. Too distracted by Parker, she hardly noticed another man standing behind him.

"How wonderful! How lucky am I to have two military men come to the rescue?" Heidi beamed an appreciative smile their way. "Why don't you grab a table? I have a breakfast casserole in the oven. I'll bring out plates in a few minutes."

Chloe's gaze lingered on Parker, hoping he'd look over his shoulder before he slipped away into the dining room. He did, and winked.

Love? she wondered. *Maybe.*

CHAPTER 12

ARKER

"Heidi said you're military?" Parker asked as he and Brad took a seat at a table near the coffee, their mugs steaming. Parker was thankful help arrived when it did or he might've been stuck outside until nightfall. The parking lot was much bigger than he gave it credit for.

"Retired now, but yes."

"Which branch?"

"Army." Brad took a sip of coffee and set it down. "You're still in." Not a question; an assessment.

"Yes. Going on six years." Parker stirred a creamer packet into his coffee. "Home on leave for a couple weeks, then back to the desert."

The conversation pinballed with the usual questions—rank, unit, duty station. For a moment, Parker forgot all about the inn and Christmas. He might as well be back in Afghanistan, enjoying a cup of coffee with a comrade before his shift started.

"You miss it?" Parker asked.

"Some days," Brad admitted. "But I prefer the change of pace. Easier to raise a family when you're not expecting to be deployed at the drop of a hat to who knows where."

Parker's lifted mug didn't make it to his lips. "Special Forces?" he guessed.

Brad nodded.

"My dad was, too. Planning to follow in his footsteps."

Brad raised an eyebrow, his gaze flicking to the kitchen door behind Parker. "What does *she* think about that?"

"Who?"

"The woman in the kitchen who looked at you with googly eyes." Brad's serious tone contrasted his humorous words. "She prepared to handle all that? Because let me tell you, it's hard on a solid marriage. But something new . . ."

Parker didn't bother to ask how Brad knew all this. *It's his training, no doubt.* "We haven't really talked about that yet." Considering they met three days ago, a conversation about the future felt rash. "It's really new. Like you said."

Brad leaned in, lowering his voice. "The military life is hard enough on a relationship. But Special Forces is something else. You're at the mercy of the mission. You can't tell her where you're going, or even how long you'll be gone. You can't always phone home to let her know you're still alive, either. The kindest thing, if you want my opinion, is to cut ties before things get too serious."

"Breakfast is finally ready," Heidi announced, carrying two heaping plates to the table.

"It smells divine, Heidi," Brad said, unwrapping silverware from a rolled cloth napkin. "You're too kind." The two exchanged a few words—about families and weather, Parker thought. But his eyes followed Chloe as she delivered plates to another table in the corner, Belle trotting at her heel.

Last night he'd dreamed about the three of them, together. As one unit.

All the doubt he'd ignored crept in as Brad's words sank in. Chloe had roots, family, and a rescue operation in Snowy Falls. For them to be together, she'd have to give it up. And for what? To sit home alone while he was in Somalia or Iraq or Libya, unable to tell her anything? That'd be cruel.

Belle spotted him and trotted to his side, demanding pats. He obliged, wishing the future he dreamt of last night could coexist alongside his army career. He'd miss Belle as much as he'd miss Chloe.

But he couldn't reconcile how it'd ever work. His commander had been right all along.

"C'mon Belle," Chloe called, flashing him a heartfelt smile before the two disappeared into the kitchen.

He cared too much about her to let her get tangled in his world.

~

CHLOE

THE DAY FLEW by in a blur between short power outages. Chloe spent much of her time in the kitchen, helping Heidi stay one step ahead of hungry guests. Parker stayed mostly outside, clearing the sidewalks after another couple of inches dusted them in the afternoon. They'd hardly seen each other in more than passing, and she realized she missed him.

"Why don't you take some supper up to him?" Heidi suggested after the last of the snickerdoodles— Chloe had never *seen* so many in one place, even at Grandma Annie's—were put away. "Everything is done in here."

Chloe plated some meatloaf with mashed potatoes and gravy. Heidi set a piece of pumpkin pie on the cover. "C'mon, Belle," Chloe chirped, as if the dog were a horse.

All day, Chloe had given more and more thought to adopting Belle, and the idea made life without her seem glum. Though she'd only witnessed one dog interaction with her at the dog park, Chloe felt confident Belle would get along with any rescue. *Just like Bandit.* She couldn't wait to tell Parker.

Upstairs, she knocked on his door, not surprised to find her butterflies in overachiever mode. She'd thought all day about kissing him again. It was more fun to think about that than uprooting her life to follow Parker. Still, it wasn't a decision they had to make now. They could take things slow, see where they might lead. Because those kisses promised it *would* lead somewhere.

"Parker?" Chloe called when there was no answer. "I brought you some supper."

Belle sniffed at the crack beneath the door, whining seconds before Chloe heard footsteps.

When the door opened, the butterflies in her stomach went berserk. She remembered the glitter on his chin yesterday. The graze of his lips. The comfort she felt in his embrace. "Hey," she greeted.

"Hey." The smile she'd come to love so much, however, was missing. "You didn't have to do that."

"Heidi insisted. We missed you at supper tonight."

Parker scrubbed a hand over the back of his neck, gaze pointed toward the floor. "Just tired is all." Finally, he took the plate. She hoped he'd open the door and invite them in, but he stood blocking the way. Even Belle grumbled her objections at being left out. "I'll take this back down to Heidi when I'm finished. Thank you."

"Roads should be cleared in the morning," Chloe added, confused and trying not to read too much into his obvious rejection. Maybe Parker *was* tired, like he said. He'd worked hard clearing snow. But her gut told her it was more. "I called Heidi's mechanic friend. The alternator made it to town right before the shop closed, so it'll get switched out first thing tomorrow."

"Good. That's good news."

"Need help wrapping gifts?"

"Already did."

Back to short responses. What little remained of Chloe's smile dropped into a frown. "Are you excited to see your family tomorrow?" she asked, desperate to fix whatever was wrong between them if only she could figure it out.

"Yes." Parker let out a heavy sigh. One that spoke more of annoyance than fatigue, if she perceived it correctly. "Look, Chloe. We can't do this."

She glanced down the hall, then back. "Do what?"

"Whatever this is between us. We can't do it. I'm sorry if I've led you on."

Chloe felt a rare loss of words as an invisible fist reached inside her chest, squeezing her heart. They'd been so happy this morning, and last night. None of this made sense. The military aspect promised challenges, but Chloe had been considering solutions all day.

"I don't understand."

"There's no future for us," he said bluntly, his icy tone making it clear that Parker didn't feel the same as she did. "I need to get some sleep."

Squaring her shoulders, Chloe managed a tight nod, even as Belle whined softly. "We'll see you in the morning, then."

"Good night." Parker closed the door, leaving her in the hallway, too shocked to move.

CHAPTER 13

 ARKER

Parker felt like a jerk.

He slept terribly, but it served him right. Lying to Chloe last night was one of the hardest things he'd ever done. He hoped to feel some semblance of relief. He was pushing her away before their feelings grew stronger. Before the pain and suffering his career path would cause took its toll on her.

Instead, he felt worse.

Empty.

Life without Chloe . . . he didn't want to picture it. It was too lonely.

Parker stared at the heap of poorly wrapped gifts,

finding his only comfort in the amusement it'd bring his family. He stuffed them one by one into the largest shopping bag and set it by the door. It was when he went back for his duffle bag that he remembered the earrings.

It didn't feel right to give them to her now. Not after the way he acted. He could leave them with Mom, and ask her to deliver them after he returned overseas.

Everything packed, Parker headed downstairs.

Chloe's bags sat near the door, leaving him to wonder whether the van was here, or if they had to walk to the autobody shop. *No sign of Belle.*

"Good morning, Parker," Heidi said with a wave from the dining room. "Chloe's already outside, loading up." She dropped her rag on the table she was wiping and came to give him a hug. "I packed some muffins and sandwiches for you two."

"Thank you, Heidi. What do I owe you?"

Heidi waved a hand. "You two more than earned your stay yesterday. It's me who owes you."

"Heidi—"

"Merry Christmas." She patted his arm. "You better help her with the bags. Safe travels."

The van was pulled up out front, the back door open. He spotted two boots and four paws beneath the open van door, and smiled until he remembered. *This is going to be a long ride home.*

"Where do you want this?" Parker asked, holding the last of Chloe's bags in offering.

"I'll take it." The twinkle in those beautiful eyes was missing, and it made him feel infinitely worse.

They worked silently, Chloe packing the van while Parker brought everything out. Between trips, he snuck in a few head scratches for Belle. At least, the dog didn't think he was a horrible human being. She was the only one out of the three of them.

"Did you say goodbye to Heidi?"

"I did."

Chloe prompted Belle to hop into the van, then closed the door. "Let's get going. I have to make a couple stops to drop off dog treats, but I promise I won't take any longer than necessary."

"Chloe—"

"Let's get you home, okay? I don't want your mom upset with me on Christmas."

Parker slipped into the passenger seat. Conflicting urges for the drive to be over and for it to never end warred as Hollandale disappeared from view. He hated this awkward tension, but to fix it would be unfair. Brad's words about avoiding a relationship at this stage in his military pursuits were too familiar. Almost an echo of the same ones his commander preached.

"Did your family make it home?" Parker asked after twenty miles of tortured silence and a failed attempt to find a radio station that wasn't mostly static.

"I don't know. No phone, remember?"

"You can use mine when we stop." It was one kindness he could offer that wouldn't cause her pain later.

"I just want to get home, okay?"

The impulse to reach for her hand was so automatic that Parker almost did. Instead, he pulled out his phone and browsed a few pictures Kaylee had texted him this morning. At least they were cuter than his sister's unveiled threat that he better not miss the ceremony tonight. Or else.

There was a text from his mom too. All about Christmas magic. She wouldn't be impressed with how he'd handled things with Chloe, but he hoped she'd understand.

Parker scrolled back to Kaylee's goofy photos of Mitzy, wanting to show Chloe but she was laser-focused on the road.

"I'm stopping in the next town," she announced after an hour of pained silence, her tone still as cool as when they left the inn. "I could use your help with Belle. I can't take her into the general store and she could use a break."

"Of course." He pivoted in his seat to face her. "Chloe—"

"Will you answer one question? *Honestly*?"

Parker tensed. He felt an ambush coming on, but was helpless to stop it. After everything, he could give her this. He owed her this much. "Yes."

"Why don't you like to talk about the army?"

He stared out the window as they entered the next town, watching each house whisk by the window. "What makes you think I don't like to talk about it?"

"You can't answer a question with a question," Chloe said flatly. "Don't pretend you don't know what I'm talking about, either. Every time I've asked you anything about the military, you give me two-word answers and shut down."

Parker hadn't realized this at all, but now that Chloe pointed it out, it forced him to confront the truth. "I don't know why I do that."

"Unacceptable, soldier," she said, rejecting his answer as she pulled into a parking spot in front of the general store. Unclipping her seat belt, she killed the engine and turned her body. She stared at him, pinning him to his seat, and he suddenly understood why Belle never questioned Chloe. Under the golden curls and sweet smile was a drill-sergeant-tough interior.

Parker found himself looking away, unable to meet her appraising gaze. He spotted a park across the street, and slipped on his coat and gloves. "I'll walk Belle," he said.

"Do you like what you do?" Chloe challenged, her hand dropping to the sleeve of his coat. He wouldn't get out of answering this one.

"Of course." But his answer lacked conviction. Even Belle, with her tilted head, seemed to question it.

"Is it what you want to do for the next decade or more? Truly?"

Parker finally shifted his gaze to match hers. This, at least, was completely true. "I'm following in my dad's footsteps. Honoring his legacy."

Chloe growled low in her throat, pushing open the door with extra force. She hopped out, slapping him with another look. "Is the army—the Special Forces—*your* dream or your dad's?" She slammed the door before he could respond. He watched her enter the store, frozen in his seat until Belle nudged his hand.

Her words held a gravity he'd never considered. He'd spent his whole life trying to live up to his dad's high standards. He knew the day he signed enlistment papers that he would do everything he could to become a Green Beret. *But is it what I really want?*

Clipping on Belle's leash, Parker stole glances of Chloe at the front counter, smiling and laughing with a woman he assumed was the store owner. "I'm proud of my service to my country," he said to Belle. "Make no mistake about that. But *my* dream"—he rested his forehead on Belle's—"includes you and Chloe."

Belle licked his cheek.

Parker felt something tight in his chest as priorities shifted for the first time in his adult life. "And yes," he murmured. "I'm talking to the dog."

 HLOE

CHLOE SPOTTED Parker with Belle the moment she left the general store. They were still in the park across the street, Parker throwing the tennis ball he'd neglected to give back to her. Had he kept it on purpose like some kind of memento?

Guilt churned in Chloe's stomach for the harsh way she acted, but her questions were fair. She'd never ask Parker to give up his military career to settle down with her in Snowy Falls. But she couldn't stand by and watch him live a lie, either. Surely, his father wouldn't have wanted that for his son.

No matter what Parker decided to do, he deserved to be happy and fulfilled.

Hand on the door handle, Chloe let out a sigh. No matter what, she couldn't finish this drive as they'd started it. She crossed the street, and headed their way.

The sight of Parker and Belle together made her yearn for a future that included the three of them. She'd yearn for it long after he returned overseas, even if they never spoke again. She wanted to believe he wanted it, too. That he was merely pushing her away to protect from some threat she couldn't understand.

"You two ready?" she called, giggling when Belle turned her head. One ear up and one ear down, nose covered in snow, the husky huffed a bark around her tennis ball. "I think she plans . . ." Chloe trailed off, her attention shifting to Parker. The moment their gazes locked, she knew something had shifted.

"You're right," he said, clipping the leash back on and gently tugging Belle toward the sidewalk.

"I'm right about what?" Two, maybe three, butterflies were awake, fluttering cautiously.

"The Special Forces was all about my dad. He wasn't an easy man to impress. Imagine getting a ninety-nine percent on a test and it *still* not being good enough. I enlisted in the army to impress him, but on his deathbed he told me it wouldn't amount to anything if I didn't do *more*."

"Do more?"

"I thought he meant the Special Forces. For years, I've clung to that belief, and it's driven every decision I've made so I could accomplish that goal. I thought it might finally be enough to impress him, even if he had to see it from heaven. My dad was a hard man, but I don't think he was heartless. Maybe he meant something different."

Chloe swallowed as Parker stepped closer, leaving very little space between them. "What are you saying, Parker?" She wanted to feel excitement, but the sting of his words last night still resonated. She had to guard her heart until she knew it was safe. Until she was *sure*.

"I'm saying I want a different path. One that includes you and Belle."

Chloe raised an eyebrow. "You figured all this out in the last ten minutes?"

"Everything with us has happened kind of fast, don't you think?" Parker hooked a finger around a curl caught in her scarf and set it free. "I mean it, Chloe. I tried to push you away because life with me in the Special Forces would've been miserable for you. It wasn't fair of me, asking you to give up everything just to follow me. Especially when it's not what I really want."

"I don't know, Parker. How's this going to work? You can't just quit the army tomorrow."

"My enlistment is up next summer, unless I extend."

Chloe's gaze dropped to his lips. "Will you?"

"No."

"Then what will you do?"

"Move home." He reached out, his arm slipping around her waist.

Her breath caught, solitary word frosting on the air between them. "Home?"

"To Snowy Falls."

Her relief and excitement too much to contain, Chloe let out a happy laugh. "But you've never even visited. How do you know you'll like it in Snowy Falls?"

"Is it anything like Hollandale?"

"Better."

"There's your answer."

"You're serious?"

Parker cupped her cheek, drawing her lips even closer. "I'm very serious. Call it Christmas magic, but I think I may very well be in love with you, Chloe Taggert." He closed the gap for a swoonworthy kiss that made the previous ones dull in comparison. This kiss held promise of a future and so much more.

"I think I'm in love with you, too," Chloe said in a breathless whisper when their lips broke apart. The dog let out a rare bark, her tail wagging in earnest. "Guess we better get you to that tree lighting ceremony."

 ARKER

"I THINK I see them over there," Chloe said, pointing toward the massive evergreen standing in the center of the downtown strip.

Parker followed her finger, spotting Mom, Bailey, and Kaylee huddled together, Styrofoam cups in their gloved hands. The sight of his family all together in one place warmed him to the core. "That's them."

Chloe looped both her arms through one of his. "They're going to be so excited to see you. Especially Kaylee."

This. This is what Parker wanted his life to be— family and the woman he loved all in the same place.

He wasn't sure what the future held for him, but he was excited to find out what might come after the army. Being together was what mattered; they'd figure out the rest.

Belle zigzagged on the leash, pulling them closer to his family. Reminding him of the crazy way the three of them collided in the airport only days ago. Maybe he and Chloe could partner to rescue and rehome dogs. The thought gave him an excited thrill for his future.

"Parker? Is that really you?" Mom nearly dropped her coffee, but Bailey's quick hands caught the cup before it splashed to the ground. Two strong arms wrapped him in a bear hug no army training could free him from. He gladly suffered for air as Mom rocked him. "I'm so happy you're finally home."

"It's all thanks to Chloe."

Mom finally let go, giving Kaylee a chance to throw her arms around his legs.

"Chloe, you *are* an angel," Mom said. "I can't thank you enough for looking after my son."

"Who's this?" Kaylee asked, kneeling on the ground and petting Belle. She giggled when the pup licked hot chocolate off her cheek then sniffed her cup, looking for more.

"That's Belle," Parker said.

"*This* is the escape artist responsible for every-thing, huh?" Mom said, a twinkle in her eyes as she looked between the three of them. "Still think I'm a fool about Christmas magic?"

Parker draped his arm around her shoulders and pulled her tight against him. "No, Mom. I know you're spot-on."

Touching Parker's other arm, Chloe said to him, "I see Everly. She'll have an update on my family. I'll be right back, okay?"

Parker couldn't resist the opportunity to plant a soft kiss on her lips, enjoying the wide eyes and gasps from his family. "I'll be right here if you need me." He watched her cross the street, feeling demanding gazes boring into him.

"You have something to tell us?" Bailey asked.

Parker watched as a gaggle of people approached and embraced Chloe, smiling to see that her family had made it home in time for Christmas too. "I'm moving home next summer," he told Mom.

"Home?"

"To Snowy Falls."

"But what about the Special Forces?" Bailey asked.

"That was Dad's dream, not mine. Mine—"

"Is with Chloe," Mom answered.

Belle leaned heavy against his legs and looked up at him with those big brown eyes. "And Belle," he added with a chuckle.

Mom hugged him tight again. "I can't wait to

have you home for good, Parker. To see you happy, that's all your dad and I truly ever wanted."

Chloe returned, a bright, beaming smile on her face. "They're back!" she announced.

"Even your little sister?" Parker asked, putting his arm around her shoulders and drawing her against him.

"She's not happy, but yes, Blakely made it home *not* married. Someday she'll thank us."

Married. Yes, he wanted to marry Chloe. The idea that this time next year Chloe could be his wife made him feel complete. Parker remembered the earrings, still tucked away in the van. He'd give them to her tonight, after all the family festivities.

"Look, they're about to get started!" Kaylee announced.

Parker snuck in one last kiss before the ceremony began. Against her ear, he whispered, "You're my Christmas magic. I love you, Chloe."

EPILOGUE

One year later...

HLOE

"Belle, you know better than to chew on that," Chloe scolded, catching the dog with the branch of their Christmas tree in her mouth. The ornament—plastic and mostly unbreakable—sat on the floor a few inches from her paws.

"You don't want to teach your sister bad habits, right?" Parker added, coming up behind Chloe and cupping both her shoulders. The gold band on his left ring finger still made those butterflies in Chloe's stomach flutter like crazy.

Though Parker still served in the Army Reserve, he now called Snowy Falls home. Together, they rescued and rehomed dogs. With her husband's help, Chloe was able to accommodate twice as many. It was also his encouragement that helped her expand Chloe's K9 Creations. Stores all over the state of Maine, and a dozen others in the New England area, now carried her famous peanut butter biscuits. If business kept up at this rate, she'd be able to open an official rescue facility within a year, two tops.

Chloe rehung the ornament after Belle relinquished the branch, her gaze falling to the sleeping beagle on the couch. They'd picked Daisy up last week from the Bangor airport. The experience was far less exciting than last year. "You think your sister's going to kill me?"

"Probably."

"She's perfect for Kaylee."

Parker kissed her cheek. "Let my sister decide that."

"Suppose we better get going. The tree lighting starts in half an hour."

"Then Grandma Annie's," Parker added.

"Rumor has it Will's bringing a date," Chloe added, slipping on her coat and gloves. When she reached for the leashes hanging by the front door, both dogs perked and bolted toward her.

"Your *brother*, Will? The one who's convinced all he needs is his Great Dane, Grimm? *That* brother?"

"Apparently Grimm brought them together." Chloe clipped on both leashes, handing one to Parker. After Grandma Annie's Christmas Eve celebration, they had Reindeer Monopoly and cookies at Tricia's. It promised to be a full night. She loved every minute of it.

At the door, Parker paused with his hand on the knob. "Have I told you today how much I love you?"

"Maybe once or twice."

Parker leaned in, kissing her tenderly. A year later, and Chloe still found herself lost when his lips brushed hers. "I'll tell you again, then," Parker said, resting his forehead against hers. "I love you, Chloe. I'm thankful every day that Belle mowed me down in the airport."

"Guess she knew what she was doing."

OTHER BOOKS BY JACQUELINE WINTERS

SWEET ROMANCE

Sunset Ridge Series
1 - Moose Be Love
2 - My Favorite Moosetake
3 - Annoymoosely Yours
4 - Love & Moosechief
5 - Under the Mooseltoe

Starlight Cowboys Series
1 - Cowboys & Starlight
2 - Cowboys & Firelight
3 - Cowboys & Sunrises
4 - Cowboys & Moonlight
5 - Cowboys & Mistletoe
6 - Cowboys & Shooting Stars

Stand-Alone
*Hooked on You

Christmas in Snowy Falls
*Pawsitively in Love Again at Christmas
*Pawsitively Home for Christmas

STEAMY ROMANTIC SUSPENSE

Willow Creek Series
1 - Sweetly Scandalous
2 - Secretly Scandalous
3 - Simply Scandalous

Sign up for Jacqueline Winter's newsletter to receive alerts about current projects and new releases!

http://eepurl.com/du18iz

ABOUT THE AUTHOR

Jacqueline Winters has been writing since she was nine when she'd sneak stacks of paper from her grandma's closet and fill them with adventure. She grew up in small-town Nebraska and spent a decade living in beautiful Alaska. She writes sweet contemporary romance and contemporary romantic suspense.

She's a sucker for happily ever after's, has a sweet tooth that can be sated with cupcakes. On a relaxing evening, you can find her at her computer writing her next novel with her faithful dog poking his adorable nose over her keyboard.